WANTED

A DEADLY SECRETS NOVEL

DEE
TENORIO

Entangled Publishing, LLC
2614 South Timberline Road
Suite 109
Fort Collins, CO 80525
Visit our website at www.entangledpublishing.com.

Ignite is an imprint of Entangled Publishing, LLC.

Edited by Wendy Chen
Cover design by LJ Anderson
Cover art by Dollar Photo Club

Manufactured in the United States of America

First Edition July 2015

ignite

For Sharon,
Who loves a dark tale.

Chapter One

Rick Trelane walked carefully toward the ribboned off crime scene, glad his hat shrouded him somewhat from the flashing red and blue lights of the nearby sheriff's cruisers. He glanced dispassionately at the body laying in the cramped parking lot of The Stand Off, Marketta's recently re-launched bar. Arms and legs strewn wide, the dark unseeing eyes of Brody Roberts stared at him as he came to a stop a few feet away from the grisly scene.

No surprise at all, Brody leaving one last mess for Rick to clean up.

"At least that saves me a bullet." He stifled the urge to kick the lifeless form. Brody deserved the added insult to his injury. Only his dumb ass would still come to a cop bar after being thrown out of the sheriff's department. Not that Rick thought for one second that any of the cops inside were the ones who pulled the trigger, just that Brody loved tempting fate.

Unfortunately, Sheriff Evigan would frown on kicking the dead. Of the two of them, Cade definitely had a stronger sense of morality. These days, Rick had a stronger sense of not giving a shit and he found that infinitely more satisfying.

"Saves you five, actually," The sheriff in question muttered as he came to stand beside Rick, handing him a cup of coffee as if they still did this crap every day. Hard to believe it had been over a year since the last dead body had been found in Marketta. "Six if you count the slug in the car door."

The size of the hole in the door wasn't large, so it wasn't likely it went through the victim first. Five out of six wasn't bad. Whoever had pulled the trigger hadn't been fucking around. Or… "Either they wanted it done for sure or someone panicked."

People tended to reflexively keep pulling the trigger once they got started, unable to stop even when the gun emptied out. He looked around to see where the bullet casings were marked on the ground around them. Thanks to the floodlights Henderson had already put up, it was easy to see the piles were in a relatively close grouping.

Cade followed his eye line and nodded. "No sign of a weapon so far. Had the presence of mind to take it with them."

"Has anyone checked the alley between the buildings to see if it was dumped?"

"I put a couple of the deps on it." Cade squinted one eye at the body. "Wasn't Brody one of the ones…"

"Mm-hmm." Something Rick had never been able to fully prove. It had been dark the night he'd been ambushed by Wheels of Pain, the motorcycle club that he'd worked to cut out of his hometown after leaving the military. Brody was on their payroll, but aside from the familiar scent of menthol cigarettes mixed with that damn Aqua Velva, he hadn't been able to make a legal charge for the attempt on his life. But they all knew. Brody was the type to take revenge with a sucker punch.

"Any idea who we notify about this?"

Rick used to have a general idea of who was related to whom for just about everybody in town. Times had changed, though. Brody was just one of the hundreds who'd come to the area in the last ten years. He didn't know the man's family in the slightest. But, he did know someone who would need to be told.

Shit. "Whitney."

"I was afraid of that." Of course Cade was. No one liked thinking of Whitney Peterson with the man she'd been in an on-again/off-again relationship with for years. They *liked* her. "Better it comes from you than me, don't you think?"

No. Rick shifted uncomfortably. Cade could at least pretend to be sorry about the news he was imparting. Whitney had been Rick's friend for so long, he used to think they'd slept in the same crib. She always knew his bullshit. He didn't relish telling her the man he hated—that she very well might have loved, however much Rick was disgusted by that concept—was dead.

Whatever Brody had done to Rick was one thing, but he'd never forgive what the bastard had done to Whitney. The fear on her face, the bruises he knew Brody had put on her. Yet another thing he'd never been able to prove. She'd been maddeningly silent about her time with Brody. "I'll take care of it. After." Somehow. "Rip been out yet?"

Cade accepted the change in subject without a hitch. "On her way."

After cleaning out the corruption from the county offices over the last two years, pretty much the entire town's assembly and staff had to be replaced from scratch. The new sheriff's deputies were handpicked by him and Cade personally, but the medical examiner hired out of New York had been chosen by the hospital. Thankfully, Dr. Jocelyn Ripley fit in with the sheriff's staff like a well-oiled cog. If cogs could freeze a man's balls at ten paces.

"Henderson better have gotten her coffee, too. The only one worse than you at this hour is her." Cade, Rick could understand. No man wanted to leave a warm wife on a cold night. Rip, on the other hand, just didn't seem to like people at any hour.

Well, no one but him and Cade, something no one had been able to explain. Proof the woman just loved being contrary, he guessed.

"*That* is one seriously dead guy."

Rick turned to find the tiny medical examiner carrying her trusty satchel with her under the yellow tape.

Dressed in a black baseball cap with "Coroner" stamped prominently on the front, her red hair pulled back into a ponytail and an oversize slicker with the same moniker over the front pocket, Ripley glanced over the scene blandly. "This certainly has wife-slash-girlfriend written all over it. She shoot him in the jewels, too?"

"Brody's not married," Rick replied, ignoring the speculation. That was the only bad thing about Rip—she was chatty. She loved to guess case outcomes like something out

of her favorite cop shows. Unfortunately, her theory impli-
cated Whitney, the last person he could imagine emptying a
revolver into anyone.

"Well, *someone* hates his guts." Ripley sidled carefully
toward the body, avoiding the blood pool seeping out from
under the corpse. "Not his first rodeo with a gun, I see." She
pointed to the aged linear gouge just beneath his cheek-
bone, surrounded by a faded shadow. "Do we know how this
first one happened?"

"No." Cade answered without even a flicker to his
even stare. They both had suspicions, Rick knew, but he
appreciated Cade not mentioning it.

"He used to be a deputy." Cade offered grimly.

"So *lots* of people hate his guts." Rip put her bag down
and started pulling on her gloves. "Well, *this* hater was extremely motivated. Victim's chest is swiss cheese. That
doesn't happen by accident."

Rick concentrated on his coffee. The better to ignore her
puncturing Brody's liver for body temp and time of death.
Even his hate didn't extend that far.

"As usual, Sheriff, any cause of death I give will be
preliminary—"

"Seems kind of obvious, doesn't it, Doc?" interrupted
Shane Henderson, the officer on duty who'd called in the
homicide and set up the scene. A good cop—dedicated, motivated, and instinctive—but not always the smartest when it
came to controlling his tongue.

Rip didn't even pick up her head at the other man's prod-
ding. "I leave stating the obvious to lesser minds, deputy."

Rick actually had to work to keep his lips from curling
as Henderson's smile dropped abruptly.

"As I was saying," She pivoted on the balls of her feet toward Cade. "*Likely* COD is the multiple GSWs to the torso. Can someone help me turn him, please?"

Always a glutton for Rip's punishment, Henderson stepped right up. Together they lifted him long enough for her to inspect the back of the body and lay him back down. "No obvious exit wounds, so we should have something to send to ballistics."

Cade nodded, but no one would mistake his expression for satisfaction. "Which won't tell us anything we don't already know."

Someone with some kind of grudge had fired a small caliber weapon into one of the biggest assholes in Marketta. Rick looked over and met Cade's dark gaze. He immediately saw the other conclusion neither of them could mention aloud.

Hardly anyone was going to care if this case never got solved.

· · ·

Whitney Peterson had just put the last pan of cheese omelet breads in the oven with a sigh, already dreaming of the coffee she'd been brewing for the last fifteen minutes. Better still, the minutes were ticking closer and closer to her morning date with the man who never missed her Sunday breakfasts. It wasn't a date to him, of course. He only came for the meal and a bit of conversation with his oldest friend, but she looked forward to it anyway.

Rick Trelane stopped in most days for coffee and a quick take-out meal, but he made it a point to sit with her on Sundays. Just to talk. Well, listen, anyway. Conversation wasn't Rick's strongest suit, but it felt good to be checked in on, to have someone care what she thought or felt, while she refilled coffee and rang up people stopping in for their fresh loaves. Not a romance by any stretch of the imagination, but it definitely brightened her week. And by Sunday, her week always needed brightening.

A sudden hard knock on the back kitchen door made her nearly jump out of her skin.

Deliveries never came on Sundays. Frowning, she glanced at the pot of coffee for a longing second before heading toward the steel door. On the way, she pulled the metal pipe from beside the ovens. She'd learned the hard way never to answer her door without it. "Who's there?"

"Rick."

She blinked in surprise, already dropping the pipe against the frame to unlock the heavy door. It swung outward almost of its own volition, caught easily by Rick's strong hand. The overhead light had turned on the moment he'd come within ten feet of the back door, but it was still dark out and his hat brim kept his handsome face in the shadows. Still, she'd know the shape of him anywhere. The green sheriff's department uniform, with its heavy coat and matching Stetson, should not have been sexy. Especially not with the gold and black stripes running down each side of the pants. Of course, they did emphasize the width of his shoulders, the length of his legs. The heavy muscle of his thighs…

Damn it, now she had to hold in a sigh. Thankfully, he wouldn't say anything about the blush rising on her cheeks. He never did.

He stepped forward and she instinctively moved back,

allowing him to pass into the kitchen without touching her. The cool, almost foggy fall air wafted in with him, scented with a woodsy citrus tang she tried her best not to draw deep into her lungs.

God, she hated this crush. Hated that common sense had no effect on it at all. Mostly, she hated the tinge of desperation she was so sure draped her whenever she was in his presence, which was why she took a few more seconds than strictly necessary to pull the door closed and get it locked.

Shaking her head slightly, hoping to snap herself out of her stupidity, Whitney turned and tried to inject some levity into her voice. "What brings you by so early? Your bacon hasn't even stopped oinking yet."

Rick didn't appear to be in a laughing mood. He never was anymore, but this was different than the stoicism she'd gotten used to since he'd returned from military duty. Colder. Almost as if he were there in a professional capacity, a thought that sparked a frozen knot of worry in her gut. He was still facing away from her, looking at the long metal table in front of him. She waited for him to turn and fill her in, but when he took his time about it, the knot grew jagged edges.

He shifted finally, taking the hat off his head and running his hand through his shaggy dark blond hair. He turned, catching her by surprise with the hard expression on his chiseled face. Those eyes of his, a searing blue that never failed to steal her breath, locked on her with an intensity that sent a chill down her spine. "We need to talk, Whit."

Normally, she liked it when he called her Whit. It reminded her of when they were kids, happy and unconcerned with life's problems. This time, there was no daydreaming away the seriousness. This visit could only be her niece. Dammit, Alison had hardly been in any trouble at all in the last few months. "How bad is it?"

"Depends on your perspective, but I do think it'll be a shock."

Whitney frowned. Her niece was temperamental, causing scenes only an over-passionate teenager could. Nothing she did could be a shock. Then the grim look on Rick's face suddenly made sense. *Brody*. It had to be. "What'd he do now?" And God, how had he dragged her into it?

"He's dead."

Quiet words. Which might explain why she wasn't sure if she really heard them. What she couldn't explain was how she felt about them. As if someone had punched her right in the solar plexus and swept her knees out from under her at the same time. Rick lunged forward, catching her before she hit the floor. Her short nails scraped the thick nylon of his jacket while her face nestled into the fur collar.

Vaguely, she realized he was carrying her, which was not a good idea since he'd only been off his cane for a few months. She tried to struggle, but he shushed her and slid her into the chair she kept by the recipe nook.

"Shit, I'm sorry. Should have worded that better." He grabbed her mug from its place by the coffee machine and filled it. "Where do you keep the brandy?"

"Bottom cabinet." She pointed by rote as reality started clearing up. Brody Roberts. Dead. Dead. *Dead.* No matter how many times the word echoed in her head, it didn't make any sense. "A-are y-you s-s-s-sure?"

She shook, though she wasn't cold, and her teeth began to chatter. Funny, with the ovens on, her bakery's kitchen was usually hot enough to make her sweat. Instead, she had goose bumps the size of Volkswagons.

He made quick work of dumping something from a bottle into the mug and then fitting the warm cup between both her hands. "Drink."

She did as she was told, keeping her eyes on him over the edge of the mug. He didn't look away and thank God, there was no pity in his gaze. "Tell me."

She had to know. Had to be sure the nightmare was truly over.

He nodded. "Saw him myself. He's not coming back this time."

She blinked. Tried to nod back at him. Then thrust the mug into his hands and ran to the sink to retch. It was, she thought with an amused sense of detachment she didn't know she was capable of, an odd first choice for a woman who'd just regained her freedom.

By the time the tears began, Rick was already there, his big hand on her back, the other helping her rinse her face. He let her cry, not doing anything to make her stop or quiet the sounds she automatically muffled against his chest. Some small part of her was aware enough to be mortified, but there was little she could do to hold it all in. She couldn't even sort out what "it all" actually was. Five years of fear, of regret and sacrifice, each one heavier than the last. But one word came to mind that finally felt right. Relief. As if all the weight she'd been carrying for so long had just...fallen off.

Eventually, the torrent of emotions began to ebb and her breathing turned to uneven gasps. She wiped her eyes, lifting her face from his shirt to realize she had soaked it through. She touched it, the mortification growing exponentially.

"Oh, God, I'm so sorry—"

"It's nothing a dry towel won't take care of." His deep voice rumbled under her fingers. "Feel better?"

Yes. No. She wasn't sure at all how she felt. Except that she didn't want to leave the safety and warmth of his hold. But Rick wasn't a toucher and the fact that he was holding her like this just proved how far over the top she'd gone. She forced herself to push him away and stand on her own feet. He kept his hands on her upper arms, waiting until she stopped wavering no matter how she pushed. Eventually, though, he let go. Because he was her friend, a careful wary friend, but one she'd already trusted with her life once. She refused to take more from him.

"How about we go out into the bakery and you can tell me what happened." She turned toward the swinging door and forced her feet forward.

"You sure you can handle it?"

Not at all. "I'm sure I need to know." Which was all that really mattered. She picked up the coffee mug from the counter on her way out, determined to keep her spine straight in front of him. They circled the glass display cases to get out to her small serving area and slid into the nearest table. He sat opposite her, calm and collected, watching for any signs of further hysteria. She'd have laughed at the expectant way he held himself—arms close to his body, doing his best to reduce his size and intimidation level—except for the fact that there was no humor left in her.

Hands flat on the table, she listened as he spoke a suc-cinct picture. Five shots to the chest. Parking lot of the bar on Main Street. No signs of a struggle. No sign of the murder weapon. No clues about the assailant. No witnesses.

He pulled a small flip notebook and pen from his shirt pocket, both of which looked dainty in his long-fingered hands. "Do you know if Brody had any personal firearms? Something he might have carried on him?"

"You think someone shot him with his own gun?" She had to blink at that. If they had, the person would've had to be strong. Very strong. Or very fast.

"We don't know much at all about what happened."

Right. It had only been a few hours. He wasn't here as the friend who came to the bakery for their Sunday breakfast. He was here as a cop. She'd be smart to remember that.

"I know he had other guns than his old service revolver, but I have no idea what kind. Mostly rifles, I think. He hunted in the woods a lot. You'd be able to find out if anything is missing from his trailer. He was obsessive about his weapons."

"Yeah, I remember." The silence stretched a few beats too long. "We'll check the registrar." Again, more silence.

She finally met Rick's questioning gaze. "Was there something else?"

"Your…relationship with Brody—"

Her head shook in immediate repudiation. "What does that have to do with anything?"

"I need to know more about the nature of it." A tone that hovered just below a demand.

"The *nature* of it?" Her hands curled into knots, her voice lifting nearly an octave without her consent.

He could have done her a favor and looked away or backed off, but he didn't. He watched. And waited.

She hated when he did that. "The *nature* of it is none of your business."

"It is if he was killed because he was treating someone the same way he did you."

Shock had her mouth opening, but no words came out.

"I realize this is difficult—"

He had no idea.

"—and you obviously still have feelings for him—"

"Stop, just stop." She put her head down. "Not another word."

Thank God he did what she said, but the uncomfortable tension had her wanting to climb out of her skin. Pushing out a breath, she met his gaze with a steady one of her own, leaning toward him so he'd know she was absolutely serious about her words.

"The only feelings I have ever had for Brody Roberts involve revulsion, anger, and a whole bunch of other things I will never fully divulge to you, because I don't like thinking about it, much less speaking of it. But whatever happens from this moment on, I *never* want to hear you confuse what happened earlier as meaning I cared about him. Okay?"

His solemn nod soothed her ruffled nerves. Until he spoke. "You can't blame me for being confused. You kept taking him back—"

She jolted at the hint of accusation in his tone. "You can't think I actually *wanted* Brody in my life."

"I didn't know what to think. You refused to tell me what was going on, even when anyone with eyes could tell it was bad. Not even when the goddamn relationship was over." That was the part that made him angry, she understood. The part that hurt him.

Better to hurt him with secrets, she'd decided, than with the truth. He always wanted to protect her, no matter what she faced. It was part of why she loved him, unrequited and pointless as that love was. But some things, no one could be protected from.

"It was *never* a relationship." More like a hostage situation. Something she never wanted Rick to know about. Of course, he figured something was wrong within weeks of his return. And he responded the way he always had to any threats to her. Brody never had a chance against Rick's rage. The same way she didn't stand a chance against Brody's.

"It could have been mutual in the beginning."

Was it wrong to laugh? Even bitterly? "It wasn't. Brody was a bully. Eventually, I realized it was safer to give in than to fight him. And it was a hell of a lot safer than the alternatives." She hated admitting that, because it proved what a coward she'd been, but it was the truth. She wasn't the only woman reduced to bartering herself for the safety of her family in those years. Wheels of Pain took what they wanted and destroyed what they couldn't. She'd saved her energy for the fights she thought she could win, not realizing until it was too late that she should have fought them all. But she couldn't change the past, no matter how hard she wanted to.

Neither could Rick. She saw the angry tick of the tendon in his jaw. "You should have told me."

And have him think of her as a whore? No, thank you. It was bad enough thinking of herself that way.

"You'd just beat him up again." And again. And again. At first, Brody was the one with the advantage of dangerous allies, but Rick had taken them on without flinching. For three years he'd fought a losing war to get rid of them. It would have eventually led to someone dying because Brody refused to give up. She wouldn't have been able to survive if that someone turned out to be Rick. So, she'd kept her mouth shut. She planned to keep it that way.

"No, I would have handled it once and for all." He would have. She could see the lethal menace in his eyes even now.

"You say things like that and yet you still wonder why I don't tell you anything?" It was never Rick's responsibility to change her life. It was hers. "*I* handled it." For the past year, Brody had stayed away. It wasn't peace, but it was a damn sight better than before. "If he was interested in anyone else, I never heard about it. But I hope to God he wasn't. No one should have to deal with that."

Rick's begrudging grunt signaled his agreement of her answer. Not acceptance, but she knew better than to expect that. It was enough that he was willing to move on.

She rubbed her eyes, hating feeling adversarial with him. Arguments were something she'd learned to live with a long time ago. One didn't spend a lifetime around a man like Rick and not have to struggle to maintain autonomy from time to time. She just hated feeling as if she were on the other side of an interrogation and talking about Brody never failed to put them in that position.

Maybe because talking about Brody always involved lying to him.

"Do you know how to reach his family?"

His question startled her. He was letting it go? "As far as I knew, Brody Roberts crawled out from under a rock."

"I could have told you that, honey." He let go a heavy sigh, softly tossing the pen onto the tabletop, his big body relaxing wearily against the back of the seat. Sweet Lord, he was! Probably because he didn't want to push her any further—fine with her—but God, did he have to be so...*male* about it?

"Is it a law that you have to have the last word or is that something you do to drive me crazy?" She ran a hand over her hair, a new kind of relief firing through her system, suddenly realizing she was still wearing the kerchief that plastered her hair back from her face and good God, the hairnet still held in the rest. She'd been sitting there raging, flying from one end of her emotional spectrum to the other, the whole time looking like a mentally disturbed high school lunch lady.

Her face flamed and for the first time, Rick seemed to notice. His mouth curved, raising just the tiniest bit at the corner as she tried to find a natural reason for her hand to be up that way. The hesitation gave her away and his slowly lifting brow destroyed any attempt at playing it off, the jerk.

Just like that, all the tension between them evaporated. Damn him, he would pick the oddest moment to show his old sense of humor. Right when she was willing to stay good and mad at him, too.

She gave in, tossing a nearby napkin at him. "Shut up. You have no idea how lucky you are that your job lets you wear a hat instead of a hairnet."

"Your job lets you smell like cookies at the end of the day. You don't want to know what I come home smelling like some days."

She wrinkled her nose, able to imagine. The sheriff's department had changed considerably in the last two years, but their jobs hadn't gotten much easier. They still had more than their share of muck to wade through, from drunken bar fights to farming disputes and apparently, the occasional dead body. Sure put making bread and cookies into perspective. So, maybe she could cut some slack for both of them. "Guess you're the one who needs some coffee now, huh?"

"Wouldn't turn it down. But let me get it." He rose from the booth with a gracefulness it was nice to see he still had. He'd nearly died not too long ago, his body beaten so badly he'd needed more than a year to fully recover. Yes, she sighed in appreciation. *So sue me.* Any woman in her right mind would appreciate a man like him, even if he did make her mad enough to throw things at his head.

He took a step, turning back as if he'd forgotten something. "One more question, before I officially get off the clock."

Whitney raised her brows.

"Can you think of anyone who might have wanted to see Brody dead? Seriously enough to actually go through with it?"

She froze, honesty warring with self-preservation. Unfortunately, self-preservation wasn't something she was capable of when Rick Trelane was near. "You mean other than me?"

It almost sounded like a joke. And she could see that he almost took it like one.

She lowered her gaze to her knotted hands, letting him think whatever he liked. "The better question to ask is… who wouldn't?"

Chapter Two

An hour later, the bakery was open and breakfast was being served. Just like normal. What wasn't normal was Rick watching her every second with those damn unreadable eyes. Not that she blamed him, but it did make it near impossible to relax. Which she clearly should never do, either. Good God, what had she been thinking? She rolled her eyes at her own stupidity. Outright *telling* him to consider her a suspect.

She grabbed a coffee pot in each hand—regular and decaf—and made the rounds to the regulars eating at the tables and the counter. As usual, Rick had parked himself at the smallest table in the back corner, those long legs of his stretched out near the wall so he wasn't in anyone's way. It didn't escape her that he preferred that particular seat because he could see everyone coming and going. *You can take the man out of the military, but you can't take the military out of the man...*

The thought brought a genuine smile to her lips as she poured regular all the way to the top of his mug. No creamer, no sugar. Rick liked his octane unadulterated. Her stomach cramped just thinking about it, but then again, her usual flavored lattes were about the only thing she'd ever seen him flinch at. Until this morning…

"I'm not going to fall apart again, if that's what you're worried about." Once the initial shock had passed and she'd thrown herself back into her routine, Whitney had found her bearings. Or compartmentalized nicely, as she knew was her way of dealing. "One breakdown a day is my limit."

Rick's gaze traveled over her face and a small grin creased his cheeks. The hint of dimples showed, reminding her again of the boy he'd once been. "It never hurts to have someone take care of you for a change."

If only…

"You shouldn't tempt me," she replied more truthfully than he probably realized. "Next thing you know, I'll be sobbing all over your shirt every other day."

He shook his head, running his hand through his shaggy hair yet again, as if he still weren't used to having it that way. "You were never a crier, Whit. If anything, you take too much on your shoulders."

"Says the cauldron to the kettle."

That faint smile widened as he brought the coffee to his lips. "My shoulders are bigger."

She narrowed her eyes, tempted to throw the towel on her hip at him. "So's your fat head."

A rusty laugh escaped him, growing louder when she bumped him with her hip. It felt good to make him laugh, especially knowing hardly anyone else could. Old camaraderie, she supposed, born in both of them before the weight of the world had landed on their backs. It meant he treated her the way he always had, the girl down the street who walked to school with him every day. Hard to shut out people like that, no matter what kind of walls you put up. And Rick had some damn high walls. Speaking of…

"Your dad should be along soon." Richard Trelane, Sr. was almost as religious as his son when it came to his regimen. Every day at seven thirty, he was there for breakfast. Had been since his wife passed away five years ago. Which was why Rick always seemed to be out her bakery door no later than seven fifteen.

"I still have a few minutes."

She gave him a look he patently ignored. "You sure that leaves you enough time to wipe away your prints?"

"How else will he know I'm still alive?"

She watched him cut up and eat the last few bites of his ham steak, as if the topic were dropped. "You could stay and have some coffee with him."

Rick scowled.

"Trelane men, I swear. He won't come in any earlier because he says you know what time he'll be here. What would your mother say?"

"That I shouldn't use so much butter on my toast." He bit into the last piece he had on his plate.

"Stubborn. Both of you."

Rick's sigh wasn't exactly exasperated, but it was close. "It's just…for the best. He gets to have the son he has in his head and I don't have to disappoint him with the son he actually has."

"You're not a disappointment." She dared put her hand

on his shoulder.

He didn't shake her off. Another one of those perks among old friends. "It's better for us both this way. Trust me."

"I don't know. Sometimes I think…if I could have one more conversation with my mother, if I could look in her eyes and have her know me one more time."

"It's not the same thing, you know that." His voice had gone gravelly, that low pitch she almost felt more than heard.

"Yeah, I know." Her mother had stopped recognizing her at all more than a year before she finally succumbed to her Alzheimers. It *was* a completely different situation, one neither of the Trelanes would sufficiently explain. Maybe Richard Trelane truly didn't understand the man his son had become and wasn't willing to try to accept him as he was. Maybe Rick really had tried and come to this painful estrangement because there was no other option. But she didn't think so. "I just don't want you to have my same regrets."

His gaze flicked up to hers again, the shadows of his past so clear in his eyes she wished he would let her wrap her arms around him just once, just for a moment, the same way he'd held her. "Regrets have a way of finding us no matter what we do."

That much, she couldn't argue. Especially not after this morning.

But she'd not made it this far without some stubbornness of her own. "I'm not going to stop trying."

His expression softened, his lips parting to say…something. As if fate couldn't let her have a single moment of intimacy, they suddenly heard the shrill scream of car breaks outside the bakery. Rick was on his feet and in front of her so fast she almost missed the whirlwind of a teenager still in her pajamas and slippers barreling into the shop.

"I did it! I did it!" Alison slammed into Whitney too quickly for even Rick to stop her, her entire skinny body connecting into a hug, her fluffy blonde curls slapping Whitney in the face.

Or, she realized as she glanced over her niece's bouncing shoulder to see his mildly smug grin, he'd *let* Alison pass him by. She used her hands to gesticulate all kinds of threats behind Alison's back that he didn't even pretend to give any weight. Just as she was vowing pumpkin spiced coffee vengeance, Alison pulled back, jumping and still squealing.

"What did you do?" Whitney asked, inwardly hoping the teen hadn't painted a mural on the entire side of the house. Again.

"Art Center accepted me! I'm going to college!" Alison screamed and bounced around the room, as patrons cheered for her. Whitney was suddenly extra glad others were there to do it. It was all she could do to keep a weak smile on her face.

Rick's presence at her shoulder gave a gentle bolster as she noticed his eyes on the girl much the way one might watch a rattler. She couldn't blame him. Alison was mercurial and the last time he'd dealt with her had been after a fight between her and some of the cheerleaders at her school. "College?"

Whitney swallowed, doing her best not to give in to a second panic attack. "Hundred thousand a *year* college."

Rick digested that a moment. "Guessing her mother didn't leave that in her bag when she dropped her on your front porch."

Whitney snorted, a short laugh escaping before she realized it and covered her mouth with her hand. "Why do you only crack jokes at the worst possible moment?"

He bumped her with his arm before reaching for his hat off the table behind her. "Why do *you* keep insisting I have a sense of humor?"

She glanced down where his hat had rested, spotting the twenty and change he'd left in its place. "Maybe because I've seen your ridiculous versions of a tip. That's three times the cost of your breakfast, you idiot!" She picked up the cash, ready to shove it in his shirt pocket but he'd already backed out of her reach.

"Put it in the college fund." He neatly sidestepped Alison's continuing happy dance with ninety-year-old Ida Steffson and her barking Yorkie. He tipped his hat up on his forehead and smiled. Not the slight curve of his mouth no one else ever noticed, but a full-on, dimple-flashing, panty-melting grin.

She managed to stay standing until he turned in the doorway and walked out to his sheriff's truck. Then she slowly sank into the nearest chair and tried to calm the somersaults her stomach was doing. After a fruitless second, she gave up and fanned her face.

Some things were just worth having an extra breakdown for.

• • •

The message was waiting when he got home.

He'd come into the shrouded dark of his house, still shaking his head at Whitney's antics, thinking of little more than a hot shower and a long nap. The blinking light on the phone he kept in a tray on his bedside table completely derailed those plans.

Shana.

Just the thought of her pried open the old wound in his chest. The acid of guilt, the deeper ache of loss, of regrets. What could have been between them had disappeared years ago, but those damn regrets still tied them together even now.

He'd been so sure when he was a kid. So determined to make something of himself in the military, dreaming of marrying his girl and protecting his country, like some kind of All American 1950s war movie hero. Then, it all turned into some kind of bitter joke.

The hometown he'd adored was being strangled by the motorcycle gang no one had been able to uproot. The girl he'd loved had been forced into a relationship with a violent man because Rick hadn't been there to protect her. The unit of men who'd become his brothers overseas, was blown away in an explosion that had nearly taken him and Cade as well, burying them in a completely different way than the others. Cade had clawed his way back, but Rick... He'd had nothing to claw his way back *to*. Nothing but lost dreams and a rage that still threatened to burn him from the inside out.

And blood.

So much blood...

Gritting his teeth, he froze out the memories from his mind. Reduced himself to the barest functionality to do it. Mechanically, he shrugged out of his coat and dumped it at the foot of the bed. Tossed his hat on top of it. Undid the strap around his thigh and pulled the tongue of his gun belt loose, setting his safetied .357 on the tray by the lamp. It was quickly joined by the revolver he kept at his ankle and the knife from his other boot. Too soon, everything was put in its place. He sat on the edge of his mattress, took off his beaten black Ramblers, one by one, lining them up with slow precision next to the side of the bed. The entire time, he stared at that blinking orange light. And dreaded.

He'd still been in the hospital, awake in the darkness, when she'd slipped in to say good-bye. Neither of them turned on the light or said a word, sitting in silence while she held his hand in both of hers. There hadn't been much to say. She was safe. Free. He'd nearly died to end her ordeal. To end it for everyone in Marketta. If he had died, it would have been worth it. But he didn't want her thanks.

"Come with me." A hoarse offer, her voice shaking as the breath left her lips.

"You know I can't." Not because of the leg suspended in traction or any of the other broken bones he'd sustained against Wheels of Pain. He wasn't the boy she knew anymore. He was more shadow than man, nothing left but duty and guilt. Not even the love he'd once had for her had survived. Sadder still, she wasn't the same girl, either. Never would be again. If he followed her, he'd be a constant reminder of her past. Of what they'd lost. And she'd be the same to him.

She nodded, dropping her forehead onto their joined hands. "I don't know if I can do this."

"You can." She'd survived everything else. Freedom wouldn't be the thing that beat her. She had her son to think of. Her parents and younger sister were going with them too, part of the deal she'd made to testify not only against the gang but the mob family backing them as well. She wouldn't be facing her future alone. "This is your chance, Shana. Start over. Start new. I'll only hold you back."

She shook her head, holding tight.

"If you can't do it for yourself, do it for Jimmy."

"*Everything* I do is for Jimmy," she snapped at him.

He took the fight in her as a good sign. "Then this is just one more thing, isn't it?"

"What about you?"

The question that stopped his memory replay every time.

He hadn't had an answer for her.

Still didn't.

It had been two years since she'd left that room and he still didn't have the first clue what to do with his life. Now that all his goals were met, answers were less clear than ever. Shana knew that better than most. Saving her family—herself—used to be all she wanted. Starting over had been terrifying, but she'd done it. She'd asked for one last favor. When she needed to talk, she'd call the phone that used to be her son's emergency burner phone. Leave a message to let him know she was all right or not. A lifeline in the unknown, for both of them, because she'd known even then that he'd need a reason to keep going. So he'd stayed, healed, stood vigil.

Someday, she'd stop calling. Stop needing him. Someday soon. They both knew that, because the fear wasn't in her voice anymore. The calls were coming further and further apart. When she was finally able to stand on her own, there would be no more messages. He'd stop having a reason to wake up every day and go about a routine that didn't mean shit to anyone. His last excuse for purpose would be gone.

Or worse, she would keep calling, just to keep him going.

Dragging herself into the past time and time again, for him. A penance she didn't deserve to pay.

Acid burned his belly. It could be happening already.

He reached for the phone, selected the message and put it to his ear.

"I know it's been a while since I called. We've been busy, so it's been harder to get time to myself." She filled him in on the minutiae of raising a seven-year-old. Her parents' health. Her sister's first year in college. Mundane details he catalogued in his mind, but the bulk of his attention was on her voice alone, listening for signs.

There was no shudder anymore. No more whispering. He could sense the confidence she was probably starting to feel. Wherever Witness Protection had put her and her family, she seemed to like it. She knew better than to give any hint of her whereabouts, never even giving a name to anyone she spoke about. He knew the message wouldn't last much longer, his grip tightening on the smooth plastic phone.

"We're okay, Rick. You don't have to worry about us anymore. This is my last call. I'm ready now. And if I'm not, I'll deal with it. I know I can now. I don't expect it to be easy for either of us, but...try, okay? Don't shut everyone out. There's more to you than d—"

The beep in his ear cut her off, angering him enough to want to throw the damn thing across the room. He didn't have to hear the words to know what she meant. More to him than death.

But that was where she was wrong.

He closed the phone, settling it with a small click into the tray. This morning, he'd looked at death and hadn't cared. A man was brutally murdered and Rick hadn't cared beyond the mess he'd have to clean up. Not until he'd delivered the news to Whitney and saw the very human reaction in her eyes. The stark contrast between them was exactly why he'd told Shana to leave him behind. Why he kept his distance from his father, a man who valued life so much Rick couldn't bear to let him see how much he…didn't. Why the blank stare of Brody Roberts mocked him so very well. Because he understood death like a first language. Knew the taste and edge of it like a lover. He'd read the message that body was truly leaving and hadn't said shit about it to anyone.

Something evil had come to Marketta. Bloodthirsty and cruel, it had claimed only its first victim. There would be more. Death like that didn't stop with one. It wouldn't stop until someone *made* it stop.

It wasn't all bad. Death was at least a purpose. The only purpose he had left.

Chapter Three

"Dressing up again?"

Whitney scrunched her eyes closed. Caught. In the laundry room, no less. She stood there in her underwear, freezing, searching through the laundry for something decent to wear. By decent, she meant pretty. She turned, gasping a little at how close her niece was.

She didn't like to use the word menacing for Alison exactly, because if Whitney herself was considered a lightweight, Alison was a toothpick. Not even having reached the maximum family height of five-foot-three, she spent most of her time hovering between kid clothes and outfits better suited for the undead. Right now, her elfin face was scrubbed clean of heavy black eye makeup, and she was wearing her light blue pajamas with cartoon cat faces all over them. She shouldn't have been able to rate as anything beyond adorable, but Alison's bulldog expression demanded an answer with absolutely no recourse.

"It's four in the morning, what are you doing awake?" Because it didn't make you guilty to answer a question with a question.

Unless you were raising a suspicious teenage girl. Then *everything* made you guilty.

Alison stared at her, her dark brown eyes chock full of accusation. Arms crossed and unimpressed, it was like being bullied by an extremely displeased kitten. "I wanted to catch you before you left for the shop, so I set my alarm."

Okaaay. That was odd. "Why?"

"This is the third day in a row you've been looking at your dresses for work. You're dressing up for *somebody*."

Blurting out a laugh, Whitney turned back to her small collection of ironed items. The blue and white dress would do nicely, might even light up her eyes. She hastily pulled it down and lifted the skirt up over her head. "Of course I am. Anyone who wants to leave a tip."

She felt Alison's hands helping, pulling the back into place, helping her get the sleeves over her shoulders. Once the dress was on, she did up the zipper. Helpful as always. Too helpful, Whitney knew. Always trying to make herself indispensable, never quite believing Whitney wouldn't throw her away. Her voice was small when she asked, "You're sure that's the only reason?"

"It's not like I usually go to work in a potato sack, Al." She was starting to wonder, though, if wearing a few dresses had the girl stressed out enough to wake up before dawn.

"I know, but…"

"But what?" Whitney turned, surprised to find Alison looking at her feet. She never shied away from confrontation.

"I just don't want you to get hurt again."

Oh. "If this is about Rick—"

"It's always about Rick. He's all you *ever* think about." Alison looked up, her eyes flashing briefly.

Whitney sighed. They'd had *this* conversation a thousand times already. "Rick is my friend. That's all he's ever been. You *know* that."

Alison reached into a basket of perfectly folded clothes, needlessly fussing with the collar of a shirt.

Whitney accepted the lack of response, fluffing the back of her hair from the collar of her dress. "If I want to look nice, I'm doing it for *me*. I feel like I can breathe for the first time in years. That's worth dressing up for. As for Rick, you just don't want me talking to him because you don't like him."

"*He* doesn't like *me*," the girl corrected, not quite pouting, but close. "He acts like I'm some kind of felon."

Not exactly an untrue allegation. She *had* spent a couple of years in and out of juvenile detention centers. Rick thought Whitney was crazy for allowing a known thief in her home, but she wasn't able to turn the girl away, not when she knew the situation Alison had been in. It wasn't her fault, what she'd been born into. She'd needed a second chance, the opportunity to find the good still inside herself. It was an opportunity Whitney wished someone could offer her, but until that day came, she'd offer it to whoever needed it. At least for Alison—and Rick, whether he believed it or not—it was paying off. They just couldn't seem to see the improvements in *each other*.

"You treat him like some kind of plague." Whitney wasn't sure who started their rivalry, but she *was* tired of feeling like a referee. "He's family—"

"*I'm* family." Alison's cheeks turned red, her hands fisting in the innocent blouse. "You don't need him now that you have me but you still act like he's more important than I am. Like he's all that matters to you."

"Well, if that were true, I wouldn't find myself defending you all the time to him, would I?" She reached out, stroking her hand over Alison's hair. When she was little and Vera came to visit, she'd been so wary, so scared her mother would leave her again, petting her had been the only way Whitney had been able to keep her calm. "No one is more important to me than you. But I'm not about to turn away a friend I've had my entire life because you two don't get along."

Alison leaned away from the touch, her shoulder rising to block Whitney's hand. "Just admit you're trying to get his attention. Thinking he'll change his mind if you keep trying. You're as bad as my mother."

Lord, Vera had done a number on her daughter. "Is there a point to this or did you just want to crush my ego nice and early today?"

Alison rolled her eyes, definitely frustrated now. "Did you stop to think what would happen if you actually get what you want?"

Considering she had no expectation whatsoever of Rick suddenly falling in love with her after successfully avoiding that fate for thirty years, no, she hadn't.

"He'll ask *questions*," Alison finally answered impatiently, shoving away from the laundry machine, temper fully sparked. "Just because Brody's dead doesn't mean the truth is. Are you ready for that? Are you ready for him to know what you did?"

No. She wasn't. But… "I have no intention of living the

rest of my life in a box because of that bastard." She'd gotten rid of him for a reason.

"I guess now you won't have to," Alison replied coolly, walking out and stomping back up the back stairs. Too bad she couldn't take her words along with her.

Whitney glanced down at the dress she was wearing, feeling foolish. Worse. Unclean. She hugged herself, resisting the urge to tear the dress off. She should have been used to that feeling, to the oily slime of the secrets inside her. She never was. She hadn't been dressing for Rick—she knew not to aim for that impossible a goal—but it had occurred to her he might appreciate the change. Maybe. The only thing Alison *had* been right about was what had her reaching back and slowly pulling the zipper back down.

If he ever did notice her, how would she be able to face it if he learned the truth?

• • •

Sitting at his desk, Rick rubbed his eyes, his brain threatening to blur from looking through the pages of information on his laptop. Initial financial overview, preliminary ballistics report, preliminary medical examiner's report… Every aspect of Brody Roberts' life reduced to some profit and loss forms, all of which seemed to point out that he was an even bigger asshole than even Rick realized.

Was there anyone Roberts didn't owe? His property—land left to him by an aunt who clearly didn't know him well—was mortgaged to the hilt. Creditors had sent him to collections for thousands. If he hadn't been on the wrong end of a .22, he'd have been out on his ass in a month. Maybe less.

Picking up his coffee mug, he was about to take a drink before realizing it was empty again. Of course. Taking the cup with him, he left his office for the break room, walking through the Deputies' Den, as the new group he and Cade hired had decided to christen their area. Starting from scratch for recruits, they used their former military contacts, reaching out for people who had training, could be trusted, and were willing to take on the challenge of rebuilding a corrupt town from the inside out. Nothing a Marine liked as much as a challenge.

Just two years ago, getting a cup of coffee like this had been an exercise in jaw clenching patience. Less an office for law enforcement, it had been like walking through a boys' club for juvenile delinquents and jocks with inferiority complexes. These days, he could almost swear he was back in the barracks of basic training. There was a lot less yelling and a hell of a lot better coffee.

Don't you mean tar? He could almost hear Whitney accusing, her nose wrinkled up in distaste. She'd learned a long time ago how to make coffee strong enough for her customers, but her personal tastes ran to embarrassingly girly. Even when they were kids, she'd been the kind to give people handmade cards full of lace, hearts, and flying unicorns. If she hadn't played marbles and dodgeball like a demon, he doubted they'd have made it past second grade with their friendship intact. Nowadays, it was her teasing smiles and sly wit he had to arm himself against. Her humor snuck past his best defenses every time.

He shrugged away the thought, something he'd had to do a lot this week. Whitney cropped up in his head for just about everything lately. The voice that kept him company. Granted, it was probably because she was the only one other than Cade that he really talked to, but he'd noticed it happening more frequently and that was not good.

It's the case, he reminded himself. Brody's death was a natural connection to Whitney, so of course she'd be more present in his mind. The same way he kept thinking about the squad room and the way it used to be. Full of traitors instead of people he was almost willing to trust with his life. Things were better now. There wasn't a damn thing wrong with noticing it.

He leaned his backside against the table and took stock of who was on shift. The voice from the back had belonged to Captain Hughes, head of their Electronic Crimes department. Hughes sat where he always did, a giant of a man folded up to his desks like a grasshopper wedged in a walnut, headphones on, shoulders hunched, lost to the world. He was also the *only* member of their Computer Crimes department digging information out of the internet like a miner sifting through grains of sand.

Schraeder, one of their two Majors, was also immersed in his work. On the phone, his head bracing the receiver to his shoulder while he scribbled madly on his blotter. Rick made a mental note to drop some Post-Its on the big midwesterner's desk. Again.

Both had been referred by Rick's former Gunny and so far, they'd been rock solid. Schraeder even had some connections with several other police branches nearby.

A glance at the whiteboard on the wall told him Henderson was riding with de la Santos, a female deputy on staff. Two women had been brought on at the suggestion of Cade's wife, Katrina, herself a former DEA agent. She'd rightfully pointed out that while Cade and he were busy looking for big and brawny in their recruits, they hadn't considered the need for a more feminine touch. By which she meant they needed a few more lethal specialists. Major Michaela Cantrell could literally beat the shit out of just about anyone she met and Marisol de la Santos was the best sharpshooter to come out of the Corps in the last ten years. Add in Ben Clark's experience as a former MP and Tonio Dominguez' psychology degree, and they had the beginnings of a strong team.

Rick still wasn't sure how ready he was for the team part. He'd been part of one before, a true one, each of the men of his unit bonded by fire and blood. Earning his place with those men had been a defining point in his life. Losing them… He flinched, swallowing the acid of guilt that rose whenever he was reminded of them. He couldn't even think of their voices without feeling the fire at his back. Their blood on his hands. Their faces still haunted him every night, along with their screams, the smell of their bodies burning in the sand…

"Chief!" Schraeder called Rick out of his dark reverie. Hanging up his phone, the big blond got to his feet in a hurry with a ripped piece of his blotter calendar in his hand. "We've had some developments in the Roberts homicide. Someone at the bar remembers seeing Roberts there regularly. That night, he was already in an altercation with someone the bartender called Wainwright." He handed the paper to Rick. "I ran some checks with my friends in other regions. Lucas Wainwright is a loan shark, has a pretty impressive territory throughout the Inland Empire. One guy I know has a contact in Norco. When I sent him Roberts' picture, he confirmed there's a marker out. He was into Wainwright for somewhere around two hundred grand."

That counted as a slap to the senses. "Where the hell would Brody get the collateral for something like that? He lived in a piece of shit trailer and drove an even shittier truck. No one in their right mind would give him that kind of cash."

Schraeder's mouth turned grim. "That's the other thing we need to talk about. Rumor was he was selling some back alley porn. He probably leveraged that."

Rick stared at the younger man until Schraeder took a step back. "Excuse me?"

"Uh…the motive or the porn?"

"I would think the motive is pretty self-explanatory."

Schraeder had the good sense not to belabor the problem. "It looks like Brody Roberts was involved in a porn ring, mostly hidden camera stuff. Hughes found it this morning and my contact just confirmed he was also selling DVDs out of his truck."

"And no one told me?"

"We didn't know what we were looking at when he first found the trail. We've been developing our leads, to be able to give you more definite information before we reported."

Rick acknowledged that with a grunt, already starting toward Hughes' corner. The only one of them that used multiple desks, Hughes maintained three computers and he seemed to use them all at the same time. Schraeder popped Hughes in the shoulder with the back of his hand. Hughes, his focus intent on the screen nearest him, jumped halfway out of his seat, swearing a blue streak before he realized

Rick was next to him.

He came to attention with a thud of his booted feet. "Sir."

Patience already thin, Rick opted to get right to it. "What'd you find on Roberts?"

"I did an in-depth check on all of Roberts' expenses for the past six months. I recognized a vendor he paid. It was the only instance to that company—or any similar company—in his banking record."

"Which is significant how?"

"He was paying to renew a domain, sir." Hughes paused, looking back and forth to see if they understood, continuing when he saw they didn't. "He was paying for a website, one that wasn't initiated from any of his known accounts. I've been running it down so I could be sure."

"Sure of what?"

Hughes might be a baby-faced giant, but Rick had always seen the keen intelligence in his green eyes, as well as a reluctant knowledge of some very dark things. The shadows were stronger than ever. "This site is membership only and very high priced, even for this kind of thing. The security on it is…impressive. I had to set up a dummy account from my mobile ISP just to get access to the content. The ownership is private, but if the victim had any connection to this site, he'd have a lot more money than this bank account is showing."

Money Hughes clearly couldn't find anywhere else, either. "You think Brody had hidden accounts?"

"If he was the owner of this site, he'd have to. Look at this." Hughes did some clicking around with his mouse, re-organizing the windows on his screen to show a black page with several photos captioned with individual category names. "Even if this site wasn't connected to a homicide, we need to get it torn down. *Now*.

"All of these options lead to a different page for a different fetish… It's pretty fucked up, sir." Hughes scratched the side of his head almost violently but it didn't seem to do much for his irritation. "There's a section for rape videos. They could be fake, some probably are, but not all. Not most of them." He hesitated, his voice lowering and his eyes closing. "Some of the victims look like drugged up minors."

Just like that, the twitchiness of these two was crystal clear. Not that he could blame them. Rick started to hear a swell of thunder in his own ears. "How old?"

Hughes looked up, his jaw clenching a few times before he answered. "Mostly teenagers, but there's an entire section for voyeurism on small children."

Rick had the sudden urge to be back at that crime scene, able to pump a full clip into Brody's worthless body. Without question, Hughes wished the same thing.

"We need a court order to go any further. Establish ownership, track the financials. We might even be able to get the subscribers."

"I'll call the judge." It wouldn't be a problem, being part of this murder case or not. But he'd be a moron not to see the possible suspects had just gone through the goddamn roof. Inwardly, he groaned. Some part of him had hoped there wouldn't be anyone they could pin this death on and they could all get back to their lives with one less piece of shit to deal with.

He never had been lucky.

"I gotta tell you, Chief," Hughes murmured, tossing his

headphones on his desk in disgust. "The more I see what this bastard did, the more I think whoever did him deserves a fuckin' medal."

Rick stared impassively at the screen. Row after row of categories, each picture showing the viewers what to expect. Unsuspecting people with no idea that someone sick was filming them. Using them. So many victims—

Unbidden, the memory hit. Whitney's face that morning last year when she'd asked him for a gun. So pale, the shadows under her eyes had worried him almost as much as her determination to arm herself, but she hadn't told him why. Outright refused. The hurt he'd seen in her had kept him from pushing even when he knew damn well he should have. Was this site why? Had Brody spied on her and she found out about it?

Or had it been something worse?

The ice in him cracked so hard he almost lost his footing. Not Whitney. Not her, too. Rage exploded in his blood, blistering with its force, threatening to overwhelm. It took his all not to crush the mug still in his hand.

Hold it in.

Push it back.

This was anger he couldn't afford to feel. Not now. Not ever. He pulled away from the emotions, rejecting them with a defensiveness that had become second nature years ago. Better not to feel. Necessary not to feel.

Stay frosty, kid… A joke from the past, said with a wink and a smile. It felt like a blade of fiery lightning through his body, but the violent repudiation did what it was supposed to. Snapped him back to the here and now, away from the piercing ghosts of memory.

"It's not our job to decide who gets justice and who doesn't." An important reminder to himself as well as the other two. Even if it sounded like ground glass coming out of his throat.

Hughes glanced sideways at Schraeder, who answered in a hushed tone. "That's just it, sir. I'm pretty sure this already was justice."

Not as much as there should have been. Rick thought of all the ways a man could suffer before he died. He'd been trained to know them and deliver them when necessary. Slowly. Without mercy or remorse. If Brody had truly been part of this ring, had put that look on Whitney's face — Whitney, who'd already been through a slow kind of hell and managed to hold on to her soul all the while — the bastard hadn't felt enough of them. Not nearly enough.

He shook his head slowly, holding tighter to reason. Grasping it until he finally found something he could focus on. He had a duty, still, to the people of this town. That couldn't be forgotten.

"It's not justice. Not yet. Brody couldn't pull this off by himself." That asshole was smart and he was sneaky, but he was also lazy as hell. "He never did a damn thing when he could get someone else to do it for him. I guarantee you, there are other people involved in this. If that's the case, looking for suspects is the least of our problems."

Wainwright might have had a reason to kill Brody, but so did anyone who was on this site. Anyone who loved the people on this site. And if they'd managed to figure out who owned it, who filmed it, who had any part in it…Brody might only be the first.

He saw the moment understanding hit both deputies.

"Shit," Schraeder blew out a breath, rubbing his fingers over his forehead. "We could be looking at more bodies."

Could wasn't the right word and Rick knew it. As far as he was concerned, it was just a matter of time.

• • •

Whitney wiped down a table, glad the workday was nearly over. Then, all she'd have to do was get home, check the Crock-Pot and crash on the couch for a little bit. She might even open one of those books she was always wanting to read. And while she indulged in that little fantasy, she could also have a nice glass of wine, a bowl of bonbons, and congratulate herself on her rock hard abs that never needed a workout. *Ha.*

Smiling, she barely noticed her hand slowing on the table, picturing a different, very specific set of abs. Male. Tanned, though she couldn't remember the last time she'd seen him without a shirt. Leading to a broad chest, sprinkled with golden chest hair. A strong neck, the column bitable. A squared, stubbled jaw, sinfully full lips, and blue, blue eyes smoldering just for her.

You look incredible today, he said in that silky rough tone that always made her shiver. *I was just thinking*, he continued, sauntering closer in those distracting uniform pants that were inexplicably tighter than usual. *I don't tell you the important things as much as I should.*

Important being far different than the things he usually reminded her about, like locking her doors and windows or zipping her coat when he thought she wasn't bundled up tight enough.

His hands lowered to the button on his pants, popping it free. *"You're so pretty, Whitney."*

She smiled, biting her lip to keep from giggling.

The zipper made a slow purring noise as it came down. *"You make every other woman I've ever met look like an old oven mitt."*

The laugh got past her, but she didn't care. There was no one else around anyway.

"You're so smart, too." The open zipper gaped, revealing more golden skin, the darkening trail of hair down his abdomen and not another stitch of fabric beneath. *"I love it when you argue with me about things I have no right to complain about in the first place. Like when you last had your oil changed."*

Oh, she'd just bet he did.

"I know we've only ever been friends, but that's just because I'm so intimidated by how sexy you are."

A full-on snort at that.

"I'm not kidding. You're a sex goddess, Whit. And all I want to do is show you how good I can be at worship."

Ooh, that one was actually good. His thumbs hooked into the loosened waistband at his lean hips, an enigmatic smile spreading those chiseled lips, leaving her breathless for what was coming next. He paused, stretching the anticipation. She watched his delicious shoulders flex, his arms push down and—

Her own terrified shriek snatched her out of her daydream as she spun, dishrag flying toward the hand that had touched her shoulder. The wet slap as the towel landed on the man's face had her eyes widening in horror even as her heart instantly started to slow down in relief at who it was.

Until she *really* realized who it was.

Then, all she could do was thank God he couldn't read her mind as well as he thought he did.

Rick stood there, taking a slow second before plucking the towel off with his thumb and forefinger. Those eyes she'd imagined smoldering in her daydream were now settled intently on her face for a completely different reason. Was it odd that she found the twitching of his left eye kind of adorable? "I see those self-defense lessons I gave you really stuck."

Probably better not to tell him about the pipe she almost clubbed him with last week.

"Serves you right, sneaking up on me." She wouldn't laugh. Not even a little. Especially not when his hawk-like gaze zeroed in on her twitching lips. Instead, she grabbed a few napkins from the table dispenser and held them out to him.

Grudgingly, she knew, he accepted. "A moose in full rutt could have snuck up on you. What were you doing, sleeping standing up?"

Her laugh as she moved by him could have passed for a nervous titter if she still did that kind of thing. "Probably. It's been a long day."

That was an understatement. It had been a long week. She'd had trouble sleeping since that morning in the bakery kitchen, her nightmares rushing back until they filled even the waking shadows. It had gotten so bad, she hated even trying to sleep. She stayed awake as long as she could, huddled in her living room, lights blazing. The dreams found her anyway, leaving her gasping and sobbing as she woke each morning.

Alison had become more and more protective as a result, probably what had set off the little confrontation in the laundry room that morning. The excitement about her acceptance letter had faded pretty quickly, once she started thinking about paying tuition. Then, the mood swings had started again and Whitney didn't know how long she'd have the energy to keep dealing with them.

Going home the last few days had felt a lot like throwing herself onto a floor made of eggshells. She never knew what was going to set Alison off, sending the moody teen out into the garage to blare her music and paint or worse, off into the sparse woods behind the house to brood. This morning it was a dress. Yesterday it was a friend canceling on plans to see a movie. Tomorrow it was probably going to be a scratched DVD.

Teenagers, she'd been told by a number of her patrons, could try the resolve of a rock on a good day. A kid with Alison's background and issues? Of course there would be problems. But Whitney had to keep trying. Having faith in Alison was the same as having faith in herself. They could overcome the past and every horrible thing they'd had to do to survive. She just had to be patient.

She busied herself picking up the chairs for the small tables. "So, I'm guessing you didn't come by for a face massage." She shouldn't have been surprised to hear him picking up the chairs behind her. With a head shake, she turned and sighed. "Don't you ever get tired of looking after me?"

He grunted, lifting another one, still not looking at her. "As if you've ever let me."

She rolled her eyes at that, then stopped when she took note of the stiffness of his stance. Tension radiated off him, as if he were strung tight enough to snap, too. While part of her wanted to put her arms around him and tell him whatever was wrong, it would be okay, she knew better. That was never what he wanted from her. That truth had been clear from the time she was fourteen and realized he belonged to someone else. Even if she could bring herself to try, she'd always know. He would never be hers. Not that way.

But she *was* his friend, reason reminded. His oldest, most loyal friend. That meant something to both of them. Right now, it meant she had the right to give him the grounding he needed, in a way he would accept, without crossing the wrong lines.

"Right," she replied, making sure to be as sarcastic as usual while she edged closer. "Where should I begin with all the times you gave me a choice concerning my welfare? Was it the ten years with a personal bodyguard walking me home from school? Or should we just skip to the nine o'clock patrol car going by my house every night?"

"We patrol everywhere. It's how we justify taking your tax dollars." He finally looked at her, a flicker cranky at having to defend himself. "I lived two doors down. That wasn't looking after you, it was walking the same way. Besides, my Dad would have killed me if anything had happened to you. You know you're still his favorite."

That one was hard to refute. Richard Trelane had been the neighborhood dad, playing with all the kids and teaching everyone how cars worked, fixing broken bikes, and explaining the glory of a well-organized garage to all who would pay attention. "Yeah, well, Richard had nothing to do with you beating up Corey Phillips for yanking up my skirt in sixth grade."

"I did do that, didn't I?" That won her another one of those secret smiles and she released the breath she'd been holding.

"He also didn't make you help out here at the bakery when Mom first got bad." She grabbed the broom from behind the swinging door to the kitchen and started sweeping behind the counter. Her tiredness from earlier faded a little, replaced with a little glow of happiness at being able to help him feel normal, even in this small way. Maybe she should slap him with a wet rag every time he was tense.

"I got paid for that," he reminded with a finger point, stacking the last chair.

"Eating your weight in messed up cookies is *not* getting paid." Honestly, this man and his hero complex.

"Says you," he replied just as fast. "Speaking of…" He tilted his head, brows rising meaningfully.

"Ha! I haven't messed up cookies in years. But since you clearly cannot be deterred from rescuing me, help me mop and I'll give you a box of your favorites."

He squinted an eye at her. "Which favorites?"

Whitney glanced at her display cabinet, searching for his guilty pleasures. "Looks like there's some chocolate chocolate-chip left. I could part with those and maybe a couple of the pralines." He did love his caramel, after all.

She knew she wasn't imagining the avarice glinting in his gaze then. "You're evil, Whit. Tempting a man with pralines."

There was no way to hold back the snort. "I don't have much else to tempt one with. Unless you like Crock-Pot roast beef from the freezer and instant mashed potatoes with a side of surly teenager. Then I'm the girl of your dreams."

"Alison giving you more problems?" More normal

still. Who'd have thought she'd ever be happy to hear his suspicious officer tone?

"She's just got her usual dose of teenage drama going. With my luck, she'll be out of the perfect shade of vermillion and the world will be about to end."

"Could be worse," he said, shrugging out of his coat and tossing it onto the upended chair legs along with his hat. "What if she were losing her mind over a boy?" Rolling up his sleeves, he started toward her and she had to force her mouth to stay closed. He'd broken way too many bones in that sumptuous body and he still moved like a lion on the prowl.

She never wanted to be a steak more in her life.

It took her a second, possibly three, when he came to a stop next to her and stared down, their bodies only a few inches apart, to realize he was waiting for her to get out of his way.

Scrambling back and hoping to God he didn't see her cheeks catch fire, she went back to sweeping like a mad woman. "Don't even make jokes about that. That's how Alison was born. Remember, Vera ran off with some guy she swore was the love of her life?"

His chuckle should have made her feel better but really, she was picturing hitting him with a couple more dishrags. The sound of water from the mop-sink echoed into the front. Soon enough, he was pushing out the rolling bucket with the wood handle of the mop. "Guessing that didn't work out the way good old Vera planned."

Good old Vera, my ass. "He dumped her at a gas station in Bakersfield. Love apparently only lasts about three hundred miles."

"That might just be true love to Vera," he pointed out

and she had to admit, he was probably right. Her cousin made Alison's artistic temperament seem downright normal in comparison.

"You have to start in the kitchen," she reminded him sweetly. It did not do to tell a man like Rick when he was correct. It happened far too often and no one needed that many 'I-told-you-so's in her life.

To his credit, he didn't complain. He backed up and soon enough she heard the water slosh with a few quick dips of the mop. They worked quietly for a while, her clearing the floor and sweeping under all the tables and stools. By the time he'd gotten back to the area behind the counter, she'd picked up the dust and relined all the trash cans. It was a pleasant kind of silence, something she didn't get too often. One she hated to break, but it didn't take a rocket scientist to know he was there for a reason.

She finished counting out her drawer, brooding slightly about what could have him so out of sorts, and putting the money into the deposit bag to be locked in the safe before she left. That done, she pulled out a small bakery box and began filling it with cookies. Just for fun, she threw in a sugar cookie decorated with googly-eyes and wild frosting hair all over it. She'd just finished closing the box when he came back from emptying the bucket and putting up the mop.

He looked…worn. Not from the mopping, either. It was an old kind of weariness showing on him. The same kind as on her, most likely. His was deeper, though. Probably because he'd been through things she didn't want to imagine and each one had taken its bite out of him. It was just as tempting now to touch him, offer comfort, as it had been earlier. She wished, just once, she was brave enough to find out if he'd let her.

Instead, she opted to get it out on the table. "You about ready to talk yet?"

A sideways glance. "That what all this slave labor was about? Softening me up?"

She shrugged. "I know how you work, Trelane. Unlike your buddy Cade, I can't take you out back and wrestle it out of you. So…"

"So you mop it out instead?" His sigh at least didn't sound perturbed. "You'd make a good gunnery sergeant. Just promise me I won't have to scrub floors with my own toothbrush next time I get pissy."

"I would never promise something like that." There it was, that full curve of his mouth. She felt like she deserved a medal for luring it out of him. But the dark had been there for a reason and whether she wanted to or not, she knew it had to be addressed. "What happened today, Rick?"

Damn. There it went, fading slowly into the angry clenching of his jaw and taking her little glow of happiness with it. His frown and glare were so much darker than usual. Almost…rattled. Which was ridiculous because in all their lives, Rick had never been thrown off by anything. He saw problems as hurdles. Sometimes challenging ones, but always something he could find a way to overcome. If he was bothered, *this* bothered, it had to be bad. Very, very bad.

The longer he stood silent, the more unnerved she became. She had too many fears of her own, swimming on the surface of her mind, for that to be a good thing. Why was he looking at her like that? As if he needed to talk to her about something and he didn't know what to say. Or where to start.

What had he found out?

What secrets had Brody spilled now?

Suddenly, she wasn't so sure she needed to know why he'd come. So, she did something neither of them expected. She reached out, slipping her hand over his and curving her fingers around them. He jolted at the contact, but he didn't push her away. Didn't say no.

"How about this?" She struggled to keep her voice from wavering. He didn't know anything. He couldn't know. All she had to do was stay calm. "I wasn't kidding about that gloriously overcooked roast beef back at my house. Alison's on a vegetarian kick this month, which means I'm going to have to eat that delicious prepackaged seasoning all by myself. Why don't you eat with us tonight? You'll get full, I won't get fat and then, when you're ready, we'll talk about whatever's bothering you."

He stayed silent a few more seconds, but his hand tightened on hers. It was enough to know he agreed. If only it was enough to take away the icy seed of fear taking root in her belly.

Chapter Four

The nice thing about teens, Rick had learned as an under-sheriff, was that if they hated people, they made no attempt whatsoever to hide it. That was kind of refreshing, considering how many people smiled nervously at him on a daily basis while secretly wondering if he was a walking time bomb. He didn't blame anybody for it. In fact, he went out of his way to make sure everyone kept their distance.

Except for those who couldn't be distanced no matter what you said to them.

He allowed himself a quick glance at Whitney, not comfortable looking away too long from the young girl across the table who hated his ass like it had rabies. Alison stared right back with those dark, empty eyes of hers, chewing on her vegetables as slowly and sullenly as she possibly could. Whitney never believed him, but he recognized the blankness in her cousin's daughter. Saw it in his own flat gaze every morning. Something dead and withered was in this girl, something no amount of care or affection could ever bring back to life. He didn't trust it.

He had no illusions of them ever becoming buddies. Taught by her mother to distrust cops and taught by a faulty protection system how to lie her ass off, Alison Peterson had immediately pegged him as someone she wouldn't be able to fool with her troubled little girl bullshit. Fair, really, since he'd pegged her as a venomous snake in pretty much the same amount of time.

No, the only one at that table with illusions was Whitney, because she believed there was something good in both of them.

"How goes the college hunt?" he asked, making sure to smile as if he cared beyond making the night easier on Whitney.

"Fine." Alison spoke through gritting teeth. "What brings you over tonight? No helpless, mass-murdered, commercially packaged dead animals at your house to eat?"

"Alison…" Whitney's disapproving rumble barely merited a flicker of Alison's over-mascaraed lashes. The girl speared an unsuspecting broccoli with her fork the way Ahab would a whale, glaring at him all the while.

"This roast beef isn't half as overcooked as you promised, Whit." Not his best segue, but not too bad.

Whitney's tense look eased a little. She was always a soft touch. Tougher than most people realized, but still too kind for the world he knew. She constantly accused him of being overprotective but the truth was, she needed it. Otherwise, parasites like Brody and even the kid here moved in and took advantage.

"I'll make it up to you by burning your breakfast tomorrow."

Despite Alison's extreme eye roll, his smile this time was easier. As tired as she was, she was still trying to take care of him. Just like at the bakery. The meal she'd sold so short had actually been delicious and a hell of a lot better than whatever microwave oven piece of plastic he'd have fed himself.

While the military had stripped him of any hang-ups about food, Whitney's cooking was his weakness. She'd sent care packages to him in Afghanistan and he'd grudgingly shared the muffins but not the cookies. Too many memories of her mother's bakery made him greedy for the taste of home. Of Christmas icing and grade school birthday parties, baseball fundraisers and football games… She didn't know it, but there were times Whitney's baking was the only lifeline he'd had over there.

And what had he done for her in return? He hadn't protected her. Hadn't helped much with her mother before he'd left. A few favors here and there seemed pathetically little to do for the girl who never gave up on him. And here he was now, trying to figure out how to ask her if her ex had ever violated her. Just the thought of it had bile rising in his throat.

He refused to let her see the dark thoughts in his head. "You'd allow the customers to see you serve something burned?"

"Well, it is for *you*." A goading one-armed shrug. "Trust me, they'd understand."

"Brat."

Her quiet laughter soothed the tension in his shoulders. Didn't do much for the discomfort, though. All through dinner, he'd tried to decide how he was going to approach the topic with her. The questions it stirred up were uncomfortable on multiple levels. First, she might not want to admit anything—few people had her level of pride-slash-stubbornness. Second, he didn't like how much this case was messing with how he thought about her. How he *saw* her.

Whitney had always occupied a safe place in his mind. Thinking of her as a woman, one with sexual history and secrets, bothered him. He didn't like the idea that he'd reduced a lifelong friend to only the parts of her he was willing to deal with. But he had.

How long had it been since he'd looked—*really* looked—at her? Maybe when he'd first come home and she'd arrived at his father's house with fresh bread and a smile so bright he'd almost forgotten how broken he was. Back then, had he seen the soft cloud of blonde curls? Had he noticed her eyes, how the sky blue had shadows that weren't there before? Considered at all that he liked the way her curves had filled in, giving her a feminine gracefulness that soothed even as it stirred? Had he appreciated anything about the woman she'd become, or just hung on to the girl he remembered?

He couldn't say for sure. But he did remember realizing something that day that he hadn't forgotten since. Whitney Peterson was dangerous. To his balance, to keeping his control. Just seeing her had made him hurt, made him happy, made him scared of what she'd see in return. A nearly blinding spiral of emotions he hadn't been able to shut down until she'd returned home.

She'd shaken him. But being around her—surrounded by her acceptance, by her unwillingness to treat him as anything other than the same guy she'd known her entire life—had been a temptation he couldn't ignore. Day by day, month by month, she made the weight of being *him* somehow easier to bear. So, he'd accepted the risk and kept her close. Not too close. Just…close enough.

Now, because of this fucking case, everything that made her threatening was suddenly back to the forefront and there was nothing he could do about it. Nothing he knew how to do. Good or bad, he couldn't stop looking at her. Thinking about her. *Noticing* her. Like right now. He found himself staring, taking her in and wondering what he'd overlooked all this time.

"Is something wrong?" Whitney brushed a curl off her forehead, one of her nervous grins lifting the corners of her lips.

"No, why?"

Now her cheeks were pinking and he couldn't stop the grin at her discomfort.

They both turned at the disgusted sigh from across the table. Alison's lips were turned into a sullen frown while she fussed with the food left on her plate, scooting it back and forth with the loud scraping of her fork on the plate.

"Alison," Whitney said, wincing at a particularly sharp plate screech. "Please stop that."

"Oh, I'm sorry, I didn't realize you two knew I was in the room." She stood up and took her plate with her as she headed toward the swinging door to the kitchen. "Guess those dresses worked after all."

In her silent wake, they both heard the slam of the dish in the sink and then stomping up the back stairs. A door banged shut somewhere upstairs, followed quickly by the low thrum of loud music through the floor, which hopefully indicated Alison wouldn't be back anytime soon.

A glance at Whitney found her with her elbows on the

table, both hands firmly over her face. "Well, I hope you liked dinner. I'm gonna go crawl into a deep dark hole now."

"You are not going down a hole." He nudged her arm, the way he often did, trying to get her to look at him.

"Yes, I am." Her voice stayed muffled behind her palms. "I'll dig it out in the woods, no one will ever find me." She was blushing so hard he could see the bright red going up into her hairline. No one in the world changed colors as easily as she did.

"It's not that bad." Alison's melodrama was hardly anything to get embarrassed by anymore. Whitney seemed to think otherwise, though, because she stayed behind her finger-mask. He tugged at her wrist, trying to think of something that might get her to relax. "I *like* your dresses."

Two fingers parted and one supremely aggravated eye glared at him. He could just see the flattened line of her bow lips and had the immediate impression of a very wet, very disgruntled old cat. Her eyes widened at a sound so foreign he almost didn't recognize it.

"*That's* what it takes to make you laugh?" Her hands finally slid off her face. "Me, willing to knock you into next Wednesday?"

"You have to admit… It'd be funny to watch you try." Her attempts at self-defense punches had left him feeling more tickled than threatened. That was why he'd decided to teach her to hit with a weapon instead. She couldn't land a fist, but damn could the woman swing.

"You know what?" She glared at him through narrowed lids, her thick lashes and fading blush giving her a haughty look as she leaned toward him, her voice almost husky. "One of these days, I'm going to knock you flat on your ass, Mr.

High and Mighty. Not only will you never see it coming, I'm gonna spend the rest of our lives rubbing it in."

He blinked, surprise catching him at the nearly sensual threat. It shouldn't have been one, Whitney never... Before he could stop himself, he looked her up and down, seeing the ripe lushness, the promise of sweetness, and had to swallow his very visceral response to it. As if some part of him wanted to lunge for a taste.

Her eyes widened as their gazes locked, her lips parting as awareness suddenly crackled like a live wire between them. He saw it then, the softening of her expression, the corners of her mouth curving into a cautious invitation. She leaned toward him, the movement slight, but he knew what it meant. Acceptance.

No, damn it. No! Control. He needed control. He cleared his throat, reining in the reaction so vehemently it turned his voice curt. "Not in this lifetime."

He swore inwardly when she looked away, the shutdown clearly stinging her like a door being slammed in her face. Worse, he couldn't say anything to soften the blow.

Very purposefully, he finished the food on his plate and they lapsed into an awkward silence. When he was done, he cleared the table the way his mother had taught him. Hers too, come to think of it. She picked up the platter with the meat still on it, the empty vegetable bowl and the serving utensils, silently leading the way to the kitchen. Gritting his teeth, he followed.

This room was a perfect reflection of the woman he'd known all his life. The warmth of her spirit clear in the leafy plants and hand painted details all over the room. The smells were a blend of her spices and sugar, cinnamon and...

Whitney. Something indefinably her that he would recognize anywhere. But for all the yellow curtains and blue flowers, she looked stiff and tense in her own space. Because of him.

She went back for the remaining stemware, her gaze downcast as she returned to the counter. By the time she filled the sink with hot, bubbling water, her pretending to ignore him was rubbing his nerves raw. This was not what he'd meant to do. Not at all what he meant to have happen. He'd come to talk to her, not fuck up everything with a few hasty words. Now he'd have to find a way to make it right.

Easier said than done.

She worked quietly, focusing down so hard the bubbles on the water should have popped from the pressure. Still not acknowledging him.

He stepped to her side, making sure she was aware of him. That he wasn't going away. "Walk with me."

She froze, the sloshing of water stopping abruptly. Small as she was, he could see her pride vibrating through every line of her. The last thing he wanted to do was take that away. Which he'd tell her if she'd just look at him.

"Whit."

She shook her head, going back at her scrubbing so hard it shook her whole frame. She had to be splashing her clothes but she didn't seem to care. "Just…don't."

Don't what? Don't show her he wished things could be different? She knew better than anyone how little of him was left. But still, she'd given him comfort at every turn. For her, he could dredge up some gentleness. He touched her shoulder, shook his head when she flinched away from him, but he didn't let go. He turned her until she had to face him. She took her time about it before she looked up at him, chin trembling, all but daring him to say something she didn't want to hear.

Beautiful. It wasn't a word he thought often, but as he drew in a breath, it resonated through him. *This* was what he hadn't seen. Hadn't allowed himself to see. Just how truly beautiful she was.

His throat tightened. "Walk with me."

She swallowed, resignation tightening her features, then nodded and led the way to the back kitchen door. They stopped for her to put on her coat. She headed immediately for the woods, which was an affectionate euphemism for the five acres or so of elms, boulders, and oak trees behind the old neighborhood. She walked on the moon dappled dirt path with the confidence of someone who knew the land blindfolded. He used to. Now, he took no steps for granted.

The sounds of their feet on the dirt were too loud in the silence. "I'm sorry about what I said in there."

Whitney shrugged, folding her arms tightly around herself. Steeling herself against him. He hated it. Hated this tension that kept building between them that didn't have to be there. "It doesn't matter."

Yes, it did. "I didn't mean to hurt your feelings."

Her scoff made him flinch. "Come on now, Rick. Let's be real. Of course it's meant to hurt. That's how you shut people out. Even me."

Especially her, when his mind went in directions it absolutely had no right to go. But he couldn't just say that, could he? "You're important to me." She had to know that much.

"No, I'm convenient."

"Excuse me?" Convenient? Not even close.

"You heard me. I'm here. I'm always here. The good buddy, good pal. We got carried away with the repartee and from what I can tell you haven't…" She waved her hand up and down at him, as if that were somehow going to make some sense. Then, all of a sudden it did and it was all he could do not to groan. "You haven't been with anyone since Shana was here. That's all it was."

"I haven't *been* with Shana since I was eighteen." It seemed important to say, though he wasn't sure how it helped. Nothing seemed to be helping. He felt like he was floundering in a dark ocean.

"That doesn't change how you still feel about her. Or me."

"How I still— What the hell are you talking about?"

"Look, it doesn't matter, okay? We're adults, a two-second flash of…whatever that was doesn't have to be made into a federal case. Let's go back to the house and forget about it. Okay? Okay." She started walking toward him, her intention clear to keep going past him back to the safety of her home and the blissless ignorance she seemed to think she'd find there.

Nothing could change the feelings he had for Whitney, not even his own determination not to feel anything for anyone. But he couldn't have her thinking of herself as disposable. He took hold of her arm, spinning her back his way, irrationally angry that she kept walking away. "Do you think I'd be here, having this ridiculous conversation, if you didn't matter?"

"Emotionally, you idiot." She shoved at his chest. "I'm talking about feelings. You know those things you pretend you don't have?"

He gripped both her arms, keeping her still and forcing her to see what she'd worked so hard to ignore. Because while she could be obstinate, on this he was immovable. "I'm not pretending. It's a choice, one I have to make every goddamned day. Not to feel anything. So whatever you have spinning in your head about Shana doesn't apply. It hasn't applied for a long goddamn time. Even if she were here, I wouldn't be with her. I can't be with anyone."

"Then why are *we* here? Why are you pushing this?" Damn it, he could see the shine in her eyes, the gleam of prideful tears she'd never want him to know about.

"Because *this*, you and me, it's all I have. It's what keeps me fucking sane."

She gaped at him, her disbelief almost as frustrating as her defensiveness.

"You're the only good part of my life, of what I used to be, that I can keep." Everything else was stained with blood, with regret and blame. He shook her slightly, so angry that she didn't seem to see that. "You think I'm willing to throw that away?"

"Why would you be throwing anything away?"

He reared back his head. Was she asking him… "You want to change things between us."

She sighed, pursing her lips to say something glib, he just knew it. Anything to keep him from seeing what she actually wanted or needed.

He cut her off. "You have no idea what that would do to you."

"Oh, I have a few," she grumbled, shaking her head at him. "I really wish I understood why you have it in your head that I'm the last virgin in the western hemisphere."

"That's not what I was talking about." He meant those emotions she'd been complaining about a few seconds ago. He'd destroy hers. It was what he did, no matter his intentions. No matter his desperation to protect. And losing her would finally obliterate the last pieces of him.

Her fingertips, cool from the night air, stroked his jaw, feeling like fire on his skin. Her voice, when it came, was thick with hurt. Hurt he was causing. But he couldn't loosen his hands, couldn't look away from her calm gaze or pull back from the painful balm of her hand now cupping his jaw. "I never asked you to change things. I'm not asking for anything."

But she should. She should have someone to hold her at night. Someone to lean on, who gave as much as she did, helping her carry the load, instead of adding to it.

He stared down at her face, wishing the words he wanted to say would come to him, but there were too many feelings spinning in him and all of them were confused. He needed her, needed her friendship. Needed her heart to keep him balanced. They both knew his had been burned out of him years ago. But he couldn't say that. Couldn't explain why his hands were tightening on her, pulling her closer when he should be pushing her away.

Don't love me. She never said she did, but he'd seen something in her eyes at the table. Something too inviting to name. Too dangerous to allow. The words were right there on the tip of his tongue, the flavor of them a sour acid too close to fear for him to acknowledge. "Everything I touch shatters. Everything."

Her expression softened, the compassion he craved turning her pliant in his hold. "*I'm* still here."

And that was the biggest fucking tragedy of it all.

"You shouldn't be." But damn if he could let her go. She was pressed against him now, on her toes, her chest to his, their breaths blended. All he'd have to do is bend his head down, the smallest bit and he'd taste her. He'd be able to draw in the ease she offered, drown in her sweetness, and take everything she had to give, forgetting the ugliness of what was inside him, if only for a little while. God, he was tempted. So fucking tempted.

But even he couldn't be that selfish.

Like everything else, she knew before he said a word. Her eyes closed, disappointment deadening her tone. "Don't use this as an excuse to stay away."

Guilt clawed at him with steel talons. He'd been thinking just that.

"I know you think cutting off everyone who loves you keeps you safe, keeps them safe, but it doesn't. You don't have to be alone. Your father is just waiting for you to—"

"Whit—"

"I'm going to say this, damn it, and you're going to listen to me. For once, you're going to listen!" She stayed in his hold, both hands now on his face, staring him point blank in the eyes. "Your father loves you. Not the memory of you. Not the medals you came home with, not the stories you think he wants to hear about what happened to you. He's just waiting for you to come back to him and be his son, the same way I waited for my mother to come back and be my Mom. That's all he wants.

"As for me, I will always be here for you. Just like you've been for me. Nothing has to change. So, do whatever you have to and forget this whole night happened. We'll go back to the way things were and that'll be the end of it."

"The end of it," he repeated doubtfully. She was still in his arms and much as he didn't want to admit it, she…felt good there. Disturbingly good.

She nodded.

"What about this?" He tugged her closer, making her aware of the full body contact—though how she'd forgotten, he couldn't understand. He felt like he was burning wherever she touched.

Her eyes widened, but her resolve remained the same. She immediately pulled back, extricating herself delicately. "I need my friend more than I need a lover. And last I checked, the latter was never on offer anyway." She turned and walked to her house, not once looking back to see how she'd completely spun his world on its axis.

He was there, staring after her for nearly half an hour, before he realized he never asked her about Brody.

Chapter Five

Three days. Three days that man had stayed out of the bakery. Three days she'd waited for him to turn up, getting angrier and angrier. And while everyone seemed to know it, no one was saying much about it.

No one but Richard Trelane.

Rick's father preferred his stool at the counter where he could keep in the thick of all the good gossip and stories. As far as he seemed to be concerned, the best story was Whitney and his son, despite the fact that she had told him twelve times already that nothing was wrong. Now that morning traffic had died off and left them alone, he was starting in on her in earnest.

"So, what'd he do to rile you up this bad, Honey?" Richard's pet name for her—given because he always said she was the sweetest kid he knew—did little to soothe Whitney's temper. Especially since all she could think of was how Rick had adopted using it every now and then, and how utterly different it sounded when he did. The jerk.

She attacked the top of her convection oven with her scrubbing towel. "Don't try to sweet talk me today, Richard. I'm not in the mood." Worse, the older man did nothing to hide his amusement.

Looking so much like his son didn't help, either. Those same vivid blue eyes—only Richard's tended to twinkle with mischief—were only the beginning. Same hair, same features, same stubborn ways. At least Richard's dark blond hair had the dignity to have gone mostly silver several years ago and his face had softened some thanks to a strong proclivity for sweets. Clearly, Rick's perverse sense of humor came from his father, too.

"Must be bad this time. You won't even look at me."

No, she wouldn't. "I look at you all the time."

"It's not my fault he's an idiot."

It should be someone's fault. Why not his?

"And you burned my eggs."

She finally spun, appalled at herself. "I—what?" A quick glance at the remains of the fluffy yellow scramble proved not a single singe mark. Great. *Two* Trelanes getting on her last nerve. "You need my attention *that* bad. Seriously?"

"I don't have any patients for another hour…"

"Good for you. I don't have any patience *right now*."

"Cute." Richard picked up his coffee mug and took a deep sip, toying absently with his phone. He stopped for a second, reading something before tapping out something else and shutting it off with a satisfied grin. "You're obviously upset and if I don't miss my guess, you've scoured everything in this place at least twice. So, I thought I'd offer to listen before you start scrubbing through the aluminum siding."

"At least the siding minds its own business."

"You may not realize it, but this is very much my business. It's not easy watching either of you hurt yourselves." Richard sighed, his face lined with weariness. "I know my son. You're going to have a long wait ahead if you're expecting him to change his mind about something all by himself."

She didn't want to think about that. "What makes you so sure it's Rick I'm mad at?" At the moment, Richard was doing just fine all by himself.

He smiled again. It wasn't the reassuring kind. "You didn't get this worked up even when that kid you took in got suspended for punching the Reed girl in the face."

"Yeah, well, the Reed girl had it coming." Sort of. No one really deserved a broken nose and three busted teeth. The Reed girl and the cheerleaders with her had been bullies, cornering Alison. She'd simply made the mistake of underestimating her prey.

Alison had been a crabby nightmare since the night Rick had come to dinner, which hadn't helped Whitney's mood, either. By the time Whitney got back to the house, Alison was already throwing her books at the walls of her room. That had lasted almost an hour, so by the time Whitney settled with her pillow and blankets on the recliner in the living room, the enraged thumping from her music was all that was left. Truthfully, all that noise was starting to be comforting, apart from the fact it usually meant Alison was epically pissed. At least Alison's resentful silent treatment was holding strong. Richard, on the other hand...

"So, what'd he do?"

She glared at him, completely fed up. "If you must know, it's not what he's done, it's what he's *not* doing."

Richard's brows went up.

"I should choke the both of you," she grumbled, interpreting his surprise. "He's shutting me out, Richard. Keep your mind out of the gutter."

"The gutter, my dear, has its benefits." He lifted his mug in salute before killing the last of his coffee. "If you fought dirty, you'd have had him on his knees a long time ago."

Whitney turned back to her oven, using her nail to fit the rag into a seam. "I never wanted him on his knees." Still didn't. The anger seeped out at the thought. She never wanted him brought low. Without the anger, though, all she was left with was the hurt she'd felt since walking away from him in the woods.

She loved his strength. Loved that he used it to protect others, even if the price was always so high. She just hated that he was using it to protect himself from her. *Her!* Did he think it was easy for her, baring feelings she knew he didn't share? Couldn't he have tried, just a little, to do what she asked? "I've never asked him for anything before. Not a single damn thing."

Except a gun.

She told her conscience to shut up.

Richard, at least, agreed. "Maybe you should."

She stopped scrubbing.

"A man like Rick needs a purpose. You could give him that."

"He has a purpose. He's important to this town, to these people. And he's my friend. I need my friend. Isn't that purpose enough?"

"That's not what I mean and you know it. Give him something to hold on to. Something to fight for."

She could feel Richard's stare piercing into her back. He was a lot like his son in that respect, too. But none of his pushing could change the facts any more than her pointless fantasies and girlhood wishes had. "You can't force someone to love you."

"You can show him there's a big difference between love and responsibility."

"Oh sure," she scoffed. "When all he feels for *me* is responsibility? Not your best logic."

"Now who's being stubborn?" His teasing smile felt like he was mocking her very real, very messed up situation.

"It's *not* stubbornness." It was immutable fact. "He almost died for her. How am I supposed to compete with that?"

"Maybe by realizing the only thing he lives for now is *you*?"

Whitney's mouth shut so hard her teeth clacked.

Richard stood up, tossing down a few bills from his wallet. "He doesn't come see *me* every day, Honey. Most folks say he's the coldest, toughest son of a bitch they've ever met—a fact I'm extremely proud of, I might add—but everyone knows he talks to you. Smiles at you, even. You seem to be the only one around here capable of reminding him that he's still alive. Something no one else has managed to do since he came back from the war. Not even Shana. Keep that in mind and maybe you'll see the cards aren't so stacked against you." He gestured for her to come closer and she leaned across the counter obediently allowing him the cheek kiss he never left without, then he whistled his way out of the bakery. Leaving her in a complete emotional disarray.

She sighed to herself—no one else around to sigh

to—and tried to shake off the little glow around her heart that Richard's words had created. Rick had made himself abundantly clear that her feelings were not welcome. Not wanted. Would never be returned. And didn't matter in the first place because he ignored her wishes and stayed away.

As quickly as that, she was mad again. Which was just as well because her eyes had begun to tear up and that was even more angering. It wasn't going to happen. She grabbed her rag and spray, deciding instead to tackle the tables now that the crowd was gone. She could rub her fingers raw on that instead because… "I'm not crying over you one more time, Rick Trelane. You and your stubborn, bullheaded, intractable, pain in the—"

The bell over the door rang, cutting her off. Probably Richard coming back for his keys or his phone… The thought trailed away when she saw a very different person standing there instead.

Not the sixty-something with the twinkle and slight paunch. Nope, this one wore a sturdy green Sheriff's uniform, complete with hat and heavy canvas jacket. This one had a hard jaw and enough masculinity roiling off him to hit her like a wave. The hat low on his head did nothing to lessen the anger burning in his gaze, either. She opened her mouth to say something, but no words came out. What was she supposed to say? I missed you? I'm so mad at you? Where the hell have you been?

Actually, that last one was perfect.

Before she could get the words past her teeth, though, he stormed around the store, looking around as if she were hiding a convict. When he stalked into the kitchen, her short-circuited brain finally found a gear. "What do you think you're doing?"

Rick kept looking around as if she hadn't said anything. Was she supposed to have hidden compartments behind the display cabinets? "Where is he?"

"Who?" And why? He looked angry enough to skin whoever it was.

"My father, where is he?"

"He left already, what is *wrong* with you?"

Rick stopped short, finally giving her his complete attention. She had to fight the urge to step back and swallow the lump in her throat at the look he gave her. Before she knew it, he was right in her space, tempting her to touch him. *Don't cross the line again. Don't.*

"Do you have any idea why my father would send me a picture of your ass with a message that said if I didn't want you, he was going for it?"

"He—what?" The idea was so preposterous she couldn't hold back a laugh. "He would nev—"

Rick yanked his phone out of his pocket, tapping it a few times before deftly flipping it and showing her a very clear image of her own behind, covered by the same beige, small-flowered dress she now wore, when she'd been standing by the oven she'd scrubbed earlier. Why, that sneaky, rotten brat!

She frowned up at him. "What exactly are you accusing me of, here?"

At least he had the decency to look taken aback, his eyes widening. "*You?*"

"Who else do you see here?" She crossed her arms, mimicking him when he thought he had every right to be accusing. "Why would *I* have any idea what your father is doing? Unless you think I took that picture myself?"

"Of course not."

"But you're still asking me like *I* did something. Like I *would* do something." She pushed at his chest, not that it got her anywhere, but at least the effort was made. Not willing to give up any ground, she twisted around him to give herself some space that wasn't overwhelmed by him. "So, what if your father takes an interest. He's not poaching on anything you want. You don't get to disappear for days on end without a word and then come stomping in here because you think someone else might be playing with your toys. We're not five anymore."

"Whitney." Just that. One word, but she heard everything he meant in it. *You're being irrational. You're not making any sense. Stop acting like this.*

"No." Just because she understood him didn't mean he should get away with it. "Did you think I was going to take Richard up on his offer? Or that I lured him to me with my evil baking ways, just to get back at you for ignoring me? That's pretty fast work, don't you think?

"I know, I must have slathered myself with frosting and thrown myself at a man twice my age whom I see more as a father, because I'm that lonely and pathetic. Since I can't have you, I'll go for the next best thing? Foolproof plan, right? Since you *know* how he loves frosting. Which explains why *you* rushed all the way over here to save him from me. Because that's the kind of person I am."

He just stared at her, his mouth in that flat line that always meant he wasn't about to say a word. He wasn't going to argue with her at all. He'd just let her run out of steam and tell her later how it was going to be. Because *he* made the rules in their relationship, didn't he?

Ooh, she almost wanted to hit him. "You know what? I'm not doing this. I'm not letting you get to me. You don't want me, you don't want anyone else wanting me, and you don't want me wanting anyone else, either. Well, too bad, Trelane. You don't get a say. Get out. Go back to wherever it was you were hiding from me, since I'm so damn frightening. Be scared somewhere else, we're all full up here!"

She stomped away, pushing into her kitchen and hoping like hell she'd hear the bell over the door again before she burst into tears. Damn him, damn him, damn him! Damn him more than he'd already damned himself.

And damn her too, for holding her breath, hoping against hope that the bell didn't ring.

One second.

Two.

Three.

By five, she allowed her breath to escape past her lips. Her fisted hands rested on her steel prep table, each heartbeat getting faster and faster. The sound didn't come.

If she turned and he wasn't there, she didn't know what she'd do. Cry? Break? Give up, finally? God, life would be so much easier if she could find a way to love someone else. To just let Rick go, out of her heart. Out of her life.

Easier, maybe…but emptier, too.

No right answers. That's all her life had ever been. Choices that weren't choices, just decisions and sacrifices that had to be made. No one gets their cake and eats it too. Her mother had said that so often, especially once they realized she wasn't going to get better. Was it supposed to make Whitney feel better? Get her to lower her expectations on happiness? How low were they supposed to get, exactly?

She'd asked him to forget. She'd literally asked him for nothing and he hadn't been able to do it. Now neither of them could. He'd finally sensed how she felt and she knew he'd never look at her the same. Now, he'd be careful. Distant. Pitying. Her stomach clenched so tight she sobbed.

This wasn't how it was supposed to end. It should have been him, happy somewhere, with someone he loved, so she'd know he was okay. So she wouldn't worry about him, think about him until her soul ached. So she could bury her hopes without regret. It was never supposed to be her walking away.

Now breaking her own heart was the only way to cut it clean.

Closing her eyes, she forced herself to turn. Then, all there was left to do was look for him through the large round glass window in the door and when he was gone, let him go.

Her eyes opened.

• • •

What the fuck are you doing?

Exactly what he'd told himself he wouldn't, he decided ruefully after Whitney walked away—again—every inch of her on fire with righteous anger. She was right to be pissed. He'd handled this all wrong. Not that he could think of a right way to handle it. Whatever *it* was.

He'd meant to stay away, found it perplexingly hard to do. He knew she'd be angry that he hadn't done what she'd asked. Hurt. But every time he started heading here to the bakery, he couldn't bring himself to do it. He couldn't sit there as if nothing had changed, pretending he wasn't cutting into her gentle heart every time he avoided a touch, ignored a pointed remark or turned down an offer of kindness from her. And he would. He had to.

The danger was palpable now. His awareness of her was growing exponentially. That night in the woods, he'd come too close. Too close to temptation, to what he feared might have been redemption. She'd offered him everything in that moment. Everything he knew better than to dream of. Solace. Peace. Maybe even forgiveness. She'd have given him her love and taken nothing in return. She'd have given him her soul.

And he would have devastated it.

He'd made the right decision. He knew he did. But right and wrong didn't mean shit when she was in arm's reach. The sight of her, that soft, powdery scent of cookies and sweetness that was uniquely hers, had him shaking with need. Wanting to grab her with both hands and take everything she offered. His fucking mouth was watering, wanting to know the taste of those full pink lips. Of her skin. Her sighs. He could still feel her against him, her full curves pressed flush, her softness a balm all its own.

He. Could. *Not*. Have. Her.

Keeping her out was the only way to keep everything else in. The rage that ate at him, the hunger that tore wounds in his soul trying to get out, the vengeance he would never be able to satisfy. And the guilt. God, the *fucking guilt*. It throttled him, the taste of smoke a stain he'd never be free of.

He kept his needs on a tight leash, boxing in every one of them so as to feel none. Whitney shook that box every day with her warmth and humor. With those bright eyes that still looked at him like he was worth her affection. Worth her acceptance. He wasn't. Never would be. He'd been wrong to think he could handle it. Wrong to let himself get so close and if he were any kind of decent person, he'd get the fuck away from her and never come back.

But he couldn't leave.

Giving in to his father's bait had been a feeble excuse and he knew it. Richard didn't often send him messages and this one had over-the-top written all over it, but it also gave him a way to come back to her. To see her without making a promise he couldn't keep.

As usual, she saw right through him and called him on his bullshit.

Now, here he stood, feeling like he was on the edge of a cliff about to crumble beneath his feet. His choices were clear. If he walked out, he could never walk back in. They would never be this close again. He'd have to shut her out and she'd have to do the same. She'd be Whitney, but she wouldn't be *his* Whitney, the one who knew most of his mistakes and didn't hold them against him. Who never gave up trying to reach the part of him he didn't have the heart to tell her was dead. She'd be everyone else's Whitney. Her smile wouldn't have a lifetime of shared experiences. Her words wouldn't have hidden meanings or secret jokes. She'd be gone.

Then, the Rick Trelane she knew really would be dead.

But if he stayed…

He had nothing to offer her. Nothing but eventual heartache and pain. He'd devour her, gorge on her love and passion, giving so little back she'd eventually hate him. He'd be no better than everyone else in her life that used her and then left her with nothing. The end result would be the same.

Whitney gone.

What kind of bastard would break her heart, knowing from the beginning what would happen, just for a little more time with her? For a few more moments where he felt like a human being instead of a monster.

He looked up, seeing her through the window of the kitchen door. Her back was to him, head bowed, shoulders hunched high, as if she were barely holding herself together. She needed someone to hold her. Someone to love her. Someone he could never be.

It was time to go. Before she turned around. Before she saw the temptation sizzling through him, demanding he stay. Insisting there could be a way to keep her. He felt like tinder too close to the fire. He had to go. He fucking *had* to. He had to let her go.

But she chose that moment to turn. To open her eyes. To sigh in relief that he was still there.

The choice was out of his hands.

He moved, drawn toward her like fire to air. He pushed through the kitchen door, colliding against her body and taking her mouth with a fury he couldn't have held in if God himself commanded it. The taste of her flooded him, sweetness and fire, while her body melted into him. It wasn't enough. He needed her closer. Needed her wrapped around him.

He knew his hands were rough when he picked her up, setting her on the metal table before pulling her knee over his hip, but he couldn't help it. Control had wisped to less than nothing. He heard her cry of surprise, used it to deepen the kiss until the carnality of it almost had him ripping at the fabric of her dress. She did nothing to stop him, either. Instead, she kissed him back, her desperate sounds urging him on. His fingers tightened on her hip, pushing her backward onto the table. She wrapped her arms around his neck and pulled him down with her, letting him take, demanding more, until he'd nearly climbed on the table with her.

They were both in over their heads, a realization he made only in the most muted of ways. Her thighs flanked him now, her calves a soft weight on the small of his back. Full breasts pushed against his chest, making him hate the stiff fabric of his uniform. He needed to feel all of her. Soft skin, firm and hot beneath his own. His hand found her bare thigh at his waist, the contact striking him like lightning. She must have felt the same way because she gasped, her hips bucking against him. He swallowed the sound, unable to let go, though he knew he should. This was too much. An explosion, that's what this was. A rare kind he couldn't control.

Dangerous. Too dangerous…

He pulled back, but Whitney whimpered, holding tight enough that when he straightened she came with him, refusing to let him go. Second by second, the kiss changed, from rapacious and wild, gentling slowly to the soothing caresses of her lips to his, her hands stroking over his cheeks, as if she were comforting him when she was the one who should have been afraid. Slowly, they parted, but only far enough to take a breath, her cool fingers continuing to soothe, her legs still tangled around him. He could have stayed there in her hold for a hundred years, the weight of everything for once quiet and still.

He glanced down at her lips, swollen and red, then to the

tears on her face. Repulsion had him snapping his hands off her waist. "I hurt you."

She shook her head, her hold on him tightening as he tried to step away. "You really don't recognize happiness, do you?"

That held him in place when nothing else would have. He had to brush his thumb over her lower lip, though. No matter what she said, his kiss hadn't been kind. "Because I kissed you?"

"Because you stayed."

Damn it, another tear fell. "You may come to regret that."

She nodded, her expression turning solemn. "I don't think I will."

"Whitney—"

She jumped when his phone went off in his jacket pocket. Cade's ringtone, an obnoxious rendition of reveille, might as well have sliced the air between them with an icy blast.

He swore, pulling it out. "I'm still on duty."

She nodded, but for the first time her expression was unreadable. He was still trying to figure out why—how—when he brought the phone to his ear. "Trelane."

Cade didn't waste any time with niceties. "There's a new victim. We need you out here off Broken Rock Pass."

Fuck. Cade hung up as soon as the information had been passed, meaning there was no option for avoiding it. Or delaying. "I have to go."

"I figured." Those kiss-swollen lips curved impishly. Probably because she had yet to release him.

"Whit." She seemed to think this was funny, that he was trapped by a pair of very feminine legs. Not the worst epitaph, he supposed, but not one he was going to allow.

"You have to let go."

"I will," she promised, even as she slid her hands down to the lapels of his coat. She tugged him close. "You will not pretend this didn't happen, do you understand? Do *not* make me come after you."

She would, too. Of that, he was sure. She had that set to her jaw again, the bulldog one he'd never gotten past in their lives.

He nodded. "After I finish with Cade."

"Good." She pressed a fast, hard kiss to his lips, gone before he'd even registered what she'd done. "And tell your father if I ever catch him looking at my ass again, he'll be eating the scrapings from under my oven for a month. Now go, I have a lunch rush to get ready for." A push—not a light one, either—and he was backing out of the kitchen, something that felt oddly like a real smile trying to pull at his lips.

He didn't let it get far, putting his hat back on as he walked through the bakery's front door. There was work to be done. He had to push his brain back into gear. Something grim was waiting for him, something very far removed from Whitney and what shouldn't be happening between them. Normally, resetting his thoughts to the next task wouldn't be hard, but for the first time in a long time, death wasn't the only thing on his mind.

Chapter Six

Rick had been shot down, blown up, held his own in forty-seven different firefights, and been beaten to within an inch of his life. All it took was one kiss from sweet little Whitney Peterson and he was shaking in his goddamned boots. He wasn't sure how the hell he made it to Broken Rock Pass without an accident.

The path to the scene wasn't hard to find. Broken Rock Pass was actually a dead-end road/lovers lane every teenager for the last thirty years in Marketta knew about. Boys lured girls out here because at night, the open sky above, utterly untainted by city lights, showed a galaxy of stars.

Last night, someone hadn't cared much for the view.

Inside the yellow crime scene tape sat a white Ford truck pulled all the way to the rail, where the dirt took over from the cracking asphalt. The driver's side door stood open, blood spatter clear on the glass. As Rick drew closer, he saw a man's body spread out on the ground, face down this time.

He frowned, because that wasn't the only thing different at the scene. This victim was also naked from the waist down, his pants bunched around his ankles.

"Didn't you say this was a second victim?" Rick ducked under the tape. Cade was there, watching Ripley as she checked over the body. As Sheriff, he didn't strictly have to be there to work the scene — he had staff for a reason — but there was no way he wasn't going to be part of this investigation. They'd had deaths in Marketta and the violence had been bad when he and Cade had first taken over, but they'd never had a specific murderer to hunt down. It wouldn't sit right not to be hands-on until it was over.

"No, but I'm pretty sure it's connected. With a few important differences."

They both looked at the pale bare ass laying sunny side up.

"What's with the pants?"

His friend shrugged. "Guess he thought he was here for a different kind of party."

"So, other than a dead guy outside his own vehicle, what makes you think they're linked?"

"Guy was shot six times to the upper body with a small-caliber weapon."

Rick's brain pricked. "The chest?"

"Not exactly," Ripley said, interrupting the conversation. She was watching them, wiping her bangs away from her forehead with her forearm.

"How do you *not exactly* shoot someone in the chest?"

"First you shoot him in the front a couple of times," she answered, deadpan as usual. "Then you shoot him in the back. So you have the big holes and the small holes evenly distributed."

He glared at her. She stared back at him. Damn woman wasn't intimidated by anything. "There were exit wounds this time?"

"Only two. I was being euphemistic. The two shots in the chest were pretty much point blank, if a little high. They went through and through. The ones to the back are probably lodged in the organs. I can't guarantee we're looking at the same weapon, either, but the wound size does indicate these shots could also have been fired from a .22. I'll know more when I open him up."

"We got an ID yet?"

"I don't recognize him," Cade looked at the victim's face, which was conveniently pointed their way. "Thought you might."

Rick tilted his head to see better. Blue eyes, brown hair, a touch over six feet, two-ten, two-twenty. Definitely not a native to Marketta. He didn't have the look of anyone else Rick knew, either, though there *was* something familiar. "Maybe we've arrested him? We can get the prints—"

Ripley stopped what she was writing to crab walk over to the victim's ankles. "Back in New York, we have this new-fangled investigative process for identifying vics." She patted the pants, then dug into the fabric to pull out a thick wallet. "It's called checking their pockets."

Cade chuckled. Rick refused on principle. The other snickers he heard were smart enough to stop quickly.

A quick flip of her wrist and Rip had the ID flap open. "His name is Dewar. *Jason* Dewar, lives on High Street. Ring any bells?" She looked around at the other deputies, but only got a head shake from Henderson and Cantrell. Shrugging, she put the wallet into an evidence bag and sealed it up. "At least you know his name now."

Rick didn't say anything, but that bit of information was more important than Rip realized. Whether Whitney believed him or not, he had been busy on the case the last several days. Brody did indeed have an entire network of unconnected financials, and getting into them had been a literal federal case because they were in out-of-state credit unions. Rick had to call in favors, liaise with the FBI, and make more than a few attempts to kiss ass without pissing anyone off. They'd discovered Brody had partners for his website, but it was impossible to tell how many because the payments went to unnamed accounts they were still working to untangle. If he was right about that address, they might well be looking at one of them.

He pulled the walkie off his shoulder. "Dispatch, is Captain Hughes in the den?"

A short wait, while Rick ignored Cade's curious gaze.

"Chief?"

"Didn't we run into a High Street address when you were digging into the website?"

Hughes's organized mind snapped to. "Yes, sir, it's popped up a few times, whenever they needed a physical address." He clicked off for a few seconds, but Rick knew he definitely had Cade's undivided attention now. "441 High Street, Marketta. We've been waiting on the search warrant. Did you find something new?"

Oh, they could say that. Rick looked to Rip, whose brows were up as she nodded. "Impressive, Chief. Wanna beat me at *Law and Order* now?"

"I'll call you back," he said to Hughes, replacing the

walkie to his shoulder. His glare did nothing to dampen Ripley's excitement. "It's not a game, Rip."

"Come on, I even have the *dun-dun* sound on my phone."

He shook his head, knowing she was going to do this no matter what he said. "Go ahead."

"Sucker," Cade murmured.

"I can hear you, Sheriff. Next time, you get to start."

"Won't change anything," Cade replied, smiling openly. "You never win, Rip."

"But I keep trying, that's the point." Stepping back from the body, she took a deep breath. "Okay, victim is in the car with his killer. Perp shoots him twice, point blank. Victim tries to escape, falls out of the cab. He couldn't run because his pants were down, so he trips, giving the killer the time to climb out after him, stand there—" She pointed to the marked prints in the dirt, "And fire four more times into his back while he crawls away. Then he walks back to the road and disappears to find his next victim." She lined herself up next to them, pleased enough with herself to pull out her phone and play the "dun-dun" sound with an inappropriate amount of glee.

"You have way too much fun trying to figure these things out." Cade laughed again.

"It's better than the rest of my job."

Well, they couldn't argue that. Rick stepped closer, taking a look at the prints next to the body and the spatter and smears on the door. One more look at the hamburger that used to be the vic's back, the shots grouped much tighter than on Brody's body.

"Victim was thrown against the door from the first two shots. He must've yanked the handle and fallen out then."

Poor bastard was dead and didn't know it yet. Judging by the wounds, even if he'd managed to get away, he'd have bled out long before he got back to town. "You check the passenger side?"

"Waited for you."

Rick was the point man for these types of scenes, his ability to cold-bloodedly and accurately dissect a kill unnerving to most of them. He backed up the way he came, circling the truck carefully, following the footprints Ripley hadn't taken into consideration. Wide-spaced, small, as if the person were running on the balls of their feet. Henderson was there with a processing kit already open, crouched with a pair of latex gloves extended.

Rick took them. "You dust for prints yet?"

"Just the handle. A couple of clean ones to run."

He put on the gloves, still concentrating on the ground. He pointed to the trail he'd been following. "You going to tag those?"

Henderson frowned. "Those what? There's any number of footprints here."

"Only one is coming off that truck. See the scuff marks? How fast the steps are touching the dirt, the way the prints are mostly partials and drags? The killer scrambled." He opened the door, looking inside the cab. Fine spatter across the seat, stopping in a broad shape along the back and bottom of the seat. The assailant had definitely been there when the shot happened and hadn't bothered cleaning up.

Chagrined, Henderson placed markers next to the footprints Rick pointed out. As Ripley had mentioned, they stopped at the body, then faded out when the dirt gave way to asphalt. "Once the body is gone, get the truck hauled back for a full process."

Henderson got to work, taking interior pictures as Rick came back to where Cade and Ripley waited. "She didn't follow him. She jumped out of her side and came around." The better to aim. Or maybe just the better to watch him die.

Ripley scrunched her face. "How do you know it's a woman?"

Rick tipped his chin toward the prints she'd first indicated, where the killer stood—feet planted—to fire those last shots. "She's wearing heels." The stiletto tip made a hard punctuation in the dirt.

"That doesn't mean the killer is female." At first, he thought she was still clinging to her theory, but she crossed her arms and raised both brows again in challenge. "What? I saw this a lot in New York. Cross-dressers are alive and well in California, boys. And sometimes they're so good at what they do, they get into sexual situations without the other party knowing what they are. It can get ugly when that happens."

"Isn't it usually the cross-dresser that ends up the victim in those cases?" Cade asked. Pretty astutely, Rick thought.

"Most of the time, yes, but they are capable of defending themselves, violently even, just like anyone else."

Her words flipped a switch in Rick's mind, reminding him of Whitney's pale, determined face almost a year ago, when she'd demanded he help her get a gun. Her voice when he asked if anyone she knew might seriously consider killing her ex. *You mean, besides me?*

"It'd have to be a small man for your theory to hold water, Rip," Cade continued. "Look at those prints. The shooter is dainty."

"They don't call 'em lady boys for nothing." She shrugged, their conversation continuing around Rick while a cold, ugly possibility tried to root itself in his psyche.

Whitney had a .22.

And he was almost positive she'd used it before.

"I'm not saying it's a fact, just that you don't have enough evidence to rule out an entire sex yet."

"Fair enough," Cade acknowledged with a nod. "But whoever it was, they weren't big."

"They walked out with blood all over them," Rick interjected, still thinking about those shoes. Were they Whitney's? Could she have done something like this? With the gun he'd given her?

No. The answer was primal, rooted so deep in him he couldn't begin to question it. Not Whitney. He'd seen her pushed to her limit. Brody hadn't died a year ago when Rick had given her the gun. Why would she kill him now, when they hadn't been together in all this time? It didn't make sense.

But neither did the body on the ground.

"We need to find out what this guy had to do with the website other than his address." Rick decided aloud. "Find out if there are any others."

"I hope not," Ripley replied, hugging herself as if she were cold. The sun was out, the breeze cool, but hardly strong enough to get through her canvas coat. "I've seen escalations like this. They only get worse."

"You'd call this an escalation?" Cade asked, glancing toward Rick for his opinion.

He didn't want to give it, but Cade would put all this together, anyway. Truth couldn't be hidden for long. "Definitely.

The killer is creating a ritual. Insisting on it with those torso shots. But this guy didn't come out here alone and get killed by someone who happened upon him."

"You're saying he was lured. By someone he knew."

"Or wanted to know." Ripley added in. "Whoever it was, the victim clearly had no idea he was a target until it was too late."

Which meant, if he was part of the website, he didn't recognize the killer from it. Or it might have nothing to do with the site at all. Rick took off his hat to shove his hand through his hair before slamming it back into place. "There are still too many variables."

"Too many coincidences, too," Cade agreed. "One thing we can all agree on. This killer is not done yet."

Dun-dun.

They both turned their heads to glare at Ripley, who for once blushed. "Sorry, I couldn't resist."

Rick looked down at the body, thought of his own actions earlier and sighed. Yeah, there was a lot of that going around.

. . .

Two hours later, Rick was in his office, frowning at the phone lying on his desk. The new vic was already in the morgue with Ripley. Henderson was working the rest of the collection on the car. Cantrell was busy trying to trace Dewar's movements the night before. There wasn't a damn thing he could do right now except wait for the new reports.

Or he could call Whitney.

"What'd the phone do this time?"

Rick looked up, surprised that he hadn't heard Cade enter the office. Especially since his friend was leaned up against the doorway as if he'd been there for a while. Worse, Cade looked amused. "What are you so happy about?"

"Who said I was happy?" Cade peeled himself from the wall, moving his big body into the room and closing the door with his foot before dropping into the guest chair as if he had an invitation.

"You're so happy most of the time you nauseate me." Not that Rick minded, really. He'd wanted Cade to find happiness. One of them should and Cade deserved it more than most. But it was still annoying.

"I'll make sure not to tell Trina you said that." Cade stretched his long legs in front of him and folded his hands over his stomach. "Besides, I wasn't so much happy as laughing at you."

"*So* much better." Rick tossed his pen onto the desktop. He'd much rather talk to Cade than try to sort his way through the confusion Whitney caused.

"I can't remember the last time I saw you looking un-certain. You're usually decisive enough to make computers look lazy."

Rick nodded, not wanting to admit how true that was. Whitney had him completely discombobulated and he didn't like the situation at all. He felt off balance, unsure. Any decision was likely to be a mistake. For once, he had to consider making no decision at all. Something that sounded cowardly as hell.

"If I didn't know better, I'd think a woman was involved."

Rick darted a look to his friend, but if Cade got the clue to back off, he didn't show it. Then again, he never did, the blunt bastard. "Leave it."

"Fine, I won't push."

"Because you know it won't get you anywhere."

"Because," Cade corrected with a pointedly raised finger, "I know someone else in this town will figure it out and fill me in better than you would anyway, you tight-lipped shithead."

Rick almost laughed. "Don't use your wife's pet names on me, Evigan."

Cade did laugh, then. It still sounded rusty to Rick, but he heard it so much more now than he ever had. "So, is there anything else you want to tell me about?"

Not that Rick could think of.

Cade sighed, humor dissipating into vague disappointment on his face. "I checked in with the deps. The canvassing on the Roberts case has turned up a broad list of possible suspects."

"Yeah, half the town, easily a thousand victims of his website and probably Santa Claus and the Easter Bunny, too." And none of them were going to be easy to rule out. "So far, our best bet is this Lucas Wainwright loan shark. He's a suspect in four other missing persons cases, all people who owed him too much for too long." Though, to be fair, most of those missing persons were from the Riverside/Corona area, not San Bernadino, and he hadn't been arrested for anything in the last five years. He wasn't clean, but he was smart enough to keep from getting caught. Maybe smart enough to use a woman to do his dirty work.

"There's also a few live fish in the complaints file. People fighting to get images pulled down off the site. There's a man from San Francisco, Mark Gorski, age fifty-seven, who kept writing the website, threatening to rain hellfire on them if they didn't remove his daughter's video. There's over fifty threatening emails from that guy alone. Hughes is working with a detective up there to run down his whereabouts the night Brody was shot. We'll have more on him by tomorrow."

Cade nodded at each piece of information, fingers steepled on his chest as he seemed to be waiting for something more. It was a long couple of seconds. "Another name keeps coming up, as well."

All of a sudden, Cade's surprise visit became crystal clear. "Whitney."

His friend inclined his head. "You haven't mentioned her in any of your reports."

"Because there's nothing to mention."

"Most folks have said otherwise." His intent gaze meant Cade wasn't letting this one go.

"Yeah? Like what?" Rick leaned back in his chair, crossing his arms. It'd be interesting to know what the local cowards had offered by way of accusation.

"Like Roberts had a bad thing for her. That he didn't let her say no to him."

Rick's fingers curled into his palms.

"They say he treated her pretty shitty whenever she was with him. Knocked her around some. Bad enough that she was still afraid of him, even after we took over the Sheriff's department." Cade's voice stayed even, but he looked down at his hands at that last part. He, at least, didn't like throwing around unsubstantiated conjecture. "I know she's a friend of yours—"

"She's…family." He almost said *mine*. Goddamn it.

Cade didn't miss the pause, but he only nodded. Shit.

That was definitely going to be brought up again. "She has motive, Rick. I looked her up and she has a registered .22 handgun. It uses .22LR ammo."

"I know she does. I registered her. I *got* her the goddamn gun. It doesn't mean jack shit around here. Just about everybody in this town has one just for the snakes and coyotes." Most kids in their town learned to shoot with small-caliber rifles for precisely that chore. LR, the most common ammunition out there, fits rifles and handguns. Whoever had mowed Brody down couldn't have found a broader range of possible weapons if they'd killed the son of a bitch with a plastic spork.

"We can't dismiss her." Cade's voice took on the steel implacability Rick remembered from when the other man had been his superior in the field. When they'd both been in the Afghan wilderness, injured and alone, trying to get back after the rest of their unit had been incinerated before their eyes. "We both know these murders are connected and you said yourself that the shooter from last night was a woman. I can't turn my eye from a viable suspect just because she's close to you. We've been down that road before."

Rick straightened. Cade had never leveled an accusation at him for the past, never brought up *that* day, and though the reminder felt like a knife in his ribs, he could see it hurt Cade to do it. The point needed to be made.

"Enemies are usually right in front of your face and the last person you suspect," Rick repeated one of the first lessons he'd been taught after arriving in Helmand Province. A lesson he hadn't listened to back then. He'd thought he could tell who to trust. Who to believe. A friend. A smiling face. A terrified kid, looking for help that never had a chance to free him before the world turned to fire…

But this was different.

"She's *not* a killer." He'd have known it. Been able to see it in her eyes if she'd lost that part of her soul. "Even if she could shoot Brody, there's no tie from her to this Dewar guy."

"That you know about. Have you talked to her about this murder at all? About her relationship with Roberts?"

"They didn't *have* a relationship." Whitney's words took on a sharper meaning coming from his own mouth. Angry. Possessive. *Protective*, he amended. He had every right to protect her. God knew he'd tried when Brody was alive. Time after time those efforts had been hamstrung by Whitney herself. "Brody forced his way into her life, until she forced him back out, *last year*. If she were going to kill him, she'd have done it then."

And he'd have gladly hidden the body for her. Hell, if he'd had any idea that the bastard was still anywhere around her, he'd have taken Brody out himself.

It was a strange realization to have, staring a Sheriff in the eye, but it was a truth he couldn't refute. He'd been the reason a lot of people were dead—friends and enemies alike—but each of them had been in the line of duty. Each had taken a part of him with them, until he knew there was no more room for any more blood on his hands. He was black from the rot of what he already had. But for Whitney, he would go back into the abyss without flinching.

But what if, his traitorous mind had to wonder, she'd gone in on her own? What if Brody had become a problem again, one she'd seen no other way to handle? That scar on the bastard's face had always been a sign to him that

Whitney was safe. But what if she wasn't? What if Brody had come back for more?

No. He rejected the question outright. She would have come to him. The situation now was far different than when he'd first come home. Whitney might be stubborn to the point of making him want to smash things, but when it came down to it, she relied on him as much as he did her. She knew he'd never let her down.

"She's not a killer." He'd stake his life on it.

Cade sat forward, as sharp as Rick had ever seen him. "Then you need to prove it. Because even though people don't blame her, they *are* thinking it. And it's making *sense* to them."

The truth of that statement settled between them like an anvil fallen from the ceiling. Just about everyone in Marketta had an axe to grind. Wheels of Pain had done more than abuse the town, they'd turned people against each other. Made them craven to protect their own. To date, they'd managed to keep the underlying resentments from exploding. But if people started thinking they could get away with it, Marketta would turn into a war zone all over again.

Cade hadn't come to him to accuse. He'd come to warn. To give Rick time to change the rising tide.

He drew in a calming breath. "How fast is the rumor moving?" A rumor no one in their right mind would dare suggest to *him*. Thankfully, Cade's sanity was occasionally a fluid thing.

"Right now it's mostly speculation. Word gets out about the second victim, though, folks are going to lose that sympathetic bend." Then it would get ugly.

Rick stood up, grabbing his coat off the back of his chair.

"I gotta go."

"Figured you did. Tell Whitney hi for me."

Rick nodded, jamming his hat on his head, his other hand already grabbing the keys from his pocket. He had a lot to say to Whitney. This time, he couldn't let anything get in the way.

Chapter Seven

Business was crappy all day, but Whitney was too busy wavering between being deliriously happy and nail-bitingly nervous to worry about it. Rick had kissed her. Kissed her like she was more important than air. She'd never been kissed like that and she'd never imagined it would happen with Rick. She'd hoped, of course. Fantasized. Her imagination had nothing on the man in reality. His hands on her body, the way he'd commanded her with a touch, melting her like glass in a kiln. She'd had no time for memories, no time for fear. There was only Rick and the desire he ignited in her. Yes, that was the word. For the first time, she understood what it meant to have her blood turn to fire.

It took three glasses of ice water to make that sensation fade enough to string together coherent thought. Then, unfortunately, being coherent gave way to worrying. What had they just done? Was anything going to change? Or had everything changed already?

That was the thought that scared her. He was so adamant that she'd regret what had happened. As if he'd ever hurt her. She knew the terrible things a man could do to a woman he claimed to care about. That wasn't the kind of man Rick was, no matter how dangerous he had trained to become. She trusted him so deeply it was practically encoded on her DNA. So, what did he think she would regret? The hours since he'd left trickled by, filled with more and more questions she couldn't begin to answer.

All of them thundered in her heart when she saw his truck pull into the parking space right in front of the shop. She straightened, watching with hungry eyes as he opened the truck door and climbed out, one beaten up boot at a time. He left his jacket in the cab, the tan uniform shirt drawn taut across his shoulders. The dark gold of his hair, thick and longer than she'd ever seen it, curled behind his ears while the front fell into his eyes before he smoothed it back impatiently and fit his hat firmly over it. The gold star of the sheriff's department, clipped to his belt, caught the light as he turned toward the store. His sunglasses were hiding his eyes, those gleaming mirrors telling her nothing. But the grim line of his mouth, his stubbled jaw set like stone, and his rolled up sleeves all added up to something bad. A fact he proved by walking to the other side of the counter and quietly ordering her to close the shop.

"What?" She didn't mean to laugh, to show the thread of nerves pulsing through her.

"Close the register, take care of whatever you have to as quickly as you can and lock up the store." His voice, the roughness somehow still stroking her awareness of him higher with each word, brooked no argument. "We need to talk."

"*Right* now."

He didn't acknowledge her attempt at humor.

Whitney sighed. Well, she didn't love him because he was easy. "Five minutes?"

"Two."

She gave him a look but he only shook his head at her. "Fine, but you have a lot of explaining to do."

He grunted and watched as she counted out her cash drawer and put a few items in the back freezer. Grabbing her purse and coat, she came around the counter and headed for the door. Rick beat her to flipping the sign to closed, holding the door open for her.

"I hate it when you get like this," she said to him, refusing to be cowed by the cold front he used so effectively on everyone else.

He simply stared at her, unmoving, those sunglasses reflecting her own disapproval back in her face. "Get in your car. I'll follow you home. No detours."

"Stop talking at me like I'm some criminal." She could feel his gaze like a brand on her skin.

"If you were a criminal, I wouldn't be talking to you at all. Get in your car."

If she thought it wouldn't hurt her hand, she'd have punched him in the gut the same way she used to back in first grade. Shaking her head, she walked out and waited for him to exit so she could lock the door. "There. Happy?"

"No. *Car.*"

"Jackass," she finally snapped, feeling no satisfaction at the juvenile name calling. She hated that they were reduced to one-word sentences, most of which were his commands.

None of it seemed to faze him at all. He walked her to her car on the street and waited until she had her seat belt on before he jogged back to his truck.

Maybe it made her an idiot, but she waited for him too, not turning over her engine until he was safely inside. Then, she drove the two miles to her house. She was still unlocking her front door when she felt him at her back. Unfair, she thought, how attuned her body was to his. Even angry, it was all she could do not to lean back into him. Why, when she hadn't dared touch him before the other day, she couldn't explain. She bit back a groan and pushed her door open.

Desperate for the distance he found so easily, she stepped into her living room and let him close up behind them. She dropped her purse on the sectional couch and sat down next to it in the corner seat that had pretty much become her bed. If she was going to fight with him—and God knew she was about to—she'd at least be comfortable.

Rick remained standing, quintessentially male in his hat and uniform, looking around as if she had people hiding in her walls. "What time does Alison get home from school?"

Of course he'd ask that. "Four, if she doesn't go out with her friends." That had become something of a norm for the girl in the last few months. Whitney generally saw it as improvement from Alison's previously anti-social behavior, but she had the feeling she'd welcome the interruption today. That still left her an hour of dealing with the argument Rick seemed dead set on having.

He nodded, finally taking off those damnable sunglasses and fixing her with a stare that showed nothing of what he was thinking. So, she had nothing to prepare her when he asked, "Do you know a man named Jason Dewar?"

She flinched. So hard she had trouble opening her eyes again, her hands clawing into the couch cushion as her throat closed like a trap door slammed shut. Memories—pain and muffled screams, terror colored like blood—flashed through her as hard as a slap and twice as fast. She fought to shut them out, cut them off before they overwhelmed everything else. The effort left her shuddering, grappling to keep her composure and failing miserably.

Worse, one second to the next, all the color faded from his face. His non-expression went slack and she could see the ugliness he was thinking as clear as day. "Fuck, you do."

"N-no, I d-don't." God, if she'd just had some warning. Talking about Brody, she could keep her composure purely out of habit. Everyone knew about him. Jason... Jason was something else. Something that made her want to throw up at the thought of him. Throw up and hide. She tried to cover the panic, tucking her legs under her on the couch, smoothing the fabric of her dress over her knees.

Rick fit his calloused hands gently over her fingers, holding them still, warming them from the bloodless cold that had taken over her entire body. "Whitney."

It was so hard to make herself look up, to meet his gaze. He'd crouched in front of her, still holding her hands. He knew. *No. No, no, no, no...* She looked away quickly, feeling the ground beneath her all but disappear. He was never supposed to know. Never...

He didn't want to believe what he was thinking, she could see it. He was looking to her for another explanation. But she had nothing to give him. Her mouth was too dry, her stomach roiling too hard. She never wanted him to see this. God, she'd worked so hard to make sure he never saw this...

"What the hell happened, Whit?" A hoarse question. *Why didn't you tell me?* He didn't ask it, but she could hear it all the same.

"Nothing." The word was out before she even thought it. Nothing had happened. That's what she'd been telling herself since that night. Nothing but a nightmare, a penance she'd paid for her fear and mistakes. Then, she'd made sure it would never happen again.

"Damn it, don't lie to me. I can see it all over you."

"I'm *fine*." She pushed that lie out too, so used to saying it, it almost sounded true. "You just…surprised me."

"That wasn't surprise, that was fuckin' terror."

"Watch your mouth in my house, Rick." She yanked her hands from his, tucking them into her underarms, disconcerted at having him so close when she felt so exposed. "Why are you asking me about him?"

"Tell me how you know him."

Suspicion pushed past the cloud of toxic emotions. "Why? What's going on?" She thought about his tension, remembered how he'd been called away earlier. "Is this some kind of interrogation?"

His mouth flattened, the rugged grooves on either side deepening.

"Are you saying Jason," that name alone made her nearly gag, "is dead now too?"

"I'm not saying anything. You are." He stood abruptly, finally giving her the space she thought she'd wanted. Getting it made her feel ten times more alone. "How do you know him?"

"How else would I know a pig like that? He was Brody's friend." He'd made her skin crawl. Watching her, invading her space, crowding her with his body. He made no effort to hide that he wanted her. That he thought he could take her any time he felt like it. Remembering it nauseated her worse.

"He and Brody were close?"

She nodded, unable to look at Rick right then. It wasn't fair, but his pushing her into this conversation made her blame him for how cornered she felt. She jumped when he swore. "He's dead, right? Just tell me. Give me that much."

"Yeah." His regretful tone made her look up, but she still couldn't tell what he was thinking. "He is. Same way as Brody. That's why I need to know how they knew each other. How *you* knew *them*."

Oh. She pushed a breath through her lips, trying to calm herself. Facts. Not blame. Another breath, this one a touch steadier. Never blame, not from him. She should have realized that. Still... Anything she said would be an admission, one that could change everything between them all over again. Could she risk that?

Did she have a choice?

What he puts together and what he knows for sure are two different things.

"I have no idea how they met, if that's what you're looking for. He started bringing Jason around, I guess about two years ago. They were always talking about cameras and video. That's what Jason does, he's a photographer."

"Did you ever hear anything about a website they owned?"

A website? Brody? "Brody hated computers." He didn't like anything he couldn't control absolutely.

Rick's gaze sharpened. "What about Dewar? Could he

have run a website?"

It didn't take much consideration. It was also a relief. He wasn't asking for details about that night. Maybe she could get out of this, secrets intact. "He handled his own just fine." She gave him the site address as she remembered it, watching as he took out the flip notebook and scribbled it down. "Is that it?"

He clicked his pen, put it away. The negative shake of his head made her roll her eyes and grab her pillow from the side of the couch, giving her something to strangle instead of him. His gaze darted to the folded pile of blankets where the pillow came from. "What are those for?"

"Are you asking in an official capacity?"

Nothing. Just more of that unreadable stare. Well, fine, let him be that way. She could be just as stubborn.

He glanced to the bedding again, no doubt counting the blankets. "You're sleeping down here." Not a question. An *assumption*. His being right didn't matter.

"Can't you stick to the point?"

He kept staring at the blankets. "I *am* sticking to the point."

Her jaw hurt from clenching.

"What did Dewar do to you? And don't tell me nothing."

What she wouldn't give to scream at him. To smash things the way Alison would have. She shook from the white-knuckled grip needed to hold it all inside. Because if she did that, then everything about that night would scream out with it. The shame, the self-disgust, the blame... She held on tighter. "Jason Dewar was a shitty excuse for a human being. I'm not sorry he's dead. I doubt anyone else will be, either. Is that enough? Can't we let this go now?"

"No."

"Why?" she snapped, panic driving her to sneer. "Because you just *have* to know? Because you want to blame yourself every time something bad happens to anyone on Earth?"

"Not anyone. *You,*" he snarled, finally showing a touch of his temper.

She refused to read anything into that remark. He didn't need her inventing meanings he didn't intend. "Why? I'm not special. Everyone in this town went through Hell the last ten years. We survived. Leave the past where it is."

"I can't."

"Why?" She hated asking it over and over. But why couldn't he let it go?

"Because you're a goddamned suspect!" He stalked toward the dining room, pacing back her way, looking as if he'd give anything to smash something. She wanted to refute him but reality was a cold splash in her face. She herself had told him she was worthy of suspicion. And she had pulled the trigger on Brody before…

"You're the one people think have the strongest motive for killing Brody."

Yes, she would be.

"Motive is just a reason," she answered more calmly than she felt. Her heartbeat was racing, hurt beginning its resonating throb in her chest, but the words coming out of her mouth were even and smooth as a winter lake. "There're people out there who've killed for a lot less than what Brody did to me."

"Every secret you keep is impeding this investigation, do you understand that? You're fucking lying to me, Whit. To *me.*" His hat went flying into the dining room before he turned, hands on his hips, his whole body rigid while he looked for something to destroy and found nothing to take out his wrath on. "How can I protect you if I don't know what to protect you from?"

She should be angry at him, especially when he settled for kicking the newel post at the bottom of the stairs, but she only felt a curious softening in her chest. Possibly because that thing was solid hard maple and it probably damaged him more than he did it. The rest dissipated because he was hurt. She'd hurt him, again. And she couldn't stop. Couldn't explain why.

Yes, it made her the soft touch he accused her so often of being, but she couldn't help it. He was a man born to protect and he hated not being able to do it. She wished she could make it easier for him, but the truth would hurt him far more. The truth would only make her look guiltier and she couldn't wound him that way. Couldn't dig into his reason for being and rip it right out of him. Couldn't bear for him to change the way he saw her.

"You won't just be a person of interest. Once you can be connected to Dewar, you'll be the *main* suspect and there won't be anything I can do to change it."

She sighed, refusing to let him see her temper had faded. "Why do you have to change it?" That earned her a supremely exasperated look she had actual problems not laughing at. He would not take that well. "I didn't kill Brody, Rick. I didn't kill Jason, either. I'm not a murderer, you know that and so does everyone else."

"Says anyone who has ever been the focus of a murder investigation." He looked as though he could have happily throttled her right then. But she had to believe the facts would speak for her. Facts Rick could live with. He kept his hands on his hips, prowling slowly back toward her on the couch. His piercing gaze narrowed, golden hair falling over his brow. He could have been a huge hunting cat honing in on a rabbit without the sense to run.

Her eyes widened, the impact of him affecting her the way it always did. Her body came to sharp attention, the hair on the back of her neck rising in primal awareness. She had to think to breathe, her mouth going dry with the need to taste him again. Lord, this man made her thirsty and he had absolutely no idea how much.

"Anyone can kill, if pushed too far. Even you. Maybe *especially* you."

She blinked, her instinctive hunger receding once she realized what he was saying. "You really think I would do something like this?"

"No, but I'm not stupid enough to believe you couldn't." His gaze, heated enough to make her breath stutter, coursed over her on the couch. "You're dangerous, Whitney. In ways you probably don't even understand."

What was she supposed to say to *that?*

"I know who you are, the way you think. I thought I knew most of what you've been through. I can figure you out most of the time, but you still manage to confuse the absolute shit out of me on a daily basis."

"Is that a compliment?" It didn't sound like it, but she never knew with him.

"Statement of fact. You're not as predictable as most people would like to think."

She would not squirm under that inscrutable gaze.

"Like most people wouldn't normally believe that you

shot Brody once already, but you did, didn't you? That's how you finally got rid of him. You put that gun I gave you in his face and pulled the trigger."

Her silence spoke for her. Damningly.

"Those people out there don't know that, but if you become the primary suspect, they're going to find out. Everything comes out and then it doesn't matter if you're guilty or not. Murder investigations are about what you can *prove*. Can you prove to anyone that you didn't shoot Brody a second time?"

She didn't care what anyone else thought. She cared about Rick. "You're asking if I can prove it to *you*."

"No." Any relief she might have felt at his uncompromising response didn't last long. "We need to prove it to Cade. So, you're going to answer my questions and then you're going to give me your gun and we're going to get you out of this before everyone you know decides you're a killer."

"One-track mind," she muttered, silently wishing he was on her track instead. *Story of our lives…*

"Where is it?"

"In my bedroom, top dresser drawer, where it always is." Right next to her bras and camisoles. She smiled at him, sweet enough to give him diabetes. If he was going to insist on this, he was going to pay for it.

• • •

Seething. It was the only word Rick could think of as he stalked up Whitney's staircase. He just wasn't sure who his anger was directed at: himself, Whitney, or that motherfucker who'd died too damn easy. Even that thought was too thin, because he couldn't decide if he meant Brody or Dewar. He couldn't decide on anything, damn it.

He kept his fists at his sides, ignoring the plastic crinkle of the evidence bag in his hand. *Job. Do your job.*

He didn't feel like being a cop right then. He felt like kicking the shit out of something. The truth had stared him in the face downstairs and he couldn't ignore it anymore.

Rape. The ugliest word he knew. He'd seen the damage it did, both overseas and here in Marketta, after he'd come home. Wheels of Pain had violated so many, in more ways than he could stand to think about, but what they'd done to the females of his town… It was an act that turned a person inside out, robbing them of safety, of choice, of everything that mattered to them. To who they were.

And it had happened to Whitney.

The need to make someone bleed, to tear them apart, had him shaking. She hadn't said it, would probably never confirm it, but he knew it was true. He recognized, was haunted by that bruised pain in her eyes because he hadn't wanted to face it. He hadn't wanted to admit to himself what had happened. Now it was clear as fucking daylight. He'd failed her again.

Something had happened a year ago, but she'd seemed so fragile and determined not to be, he'd been afraid to push too hard. Instead, he agreed to give her the shooting lessons she asked for. He made sure she was capable of handling the small weapon because it clearly made her feel safer. He'd done what he thought was the right thing at the time, keeping as much an eye on her as she'd allow.

He'd finally been getting back to full duty, no longer needing his cane much at all. She'd stopped allowing Brody near her and even Alison had settled down. He'd thought things were finally getting better. Then, her mother had died, but she came through it, seemingly stronger than ever. He'd let himself believe the lie, that she hadn't had to deal with the same horrors as so many others, because it was what he'd wanted to believe. It made him feel better about not being able to change her situation any more than he'd been able to help his own. He should have known. He should have fucking *known*.

He came to the top of the stairs, ruthlessly snapping himself back to the present. The job, damn it. He was there to do his job.

A job that might incriminate the one person in the world he had left to protect.

He closed his eyes, took a deep breath. *Focus*. This was the way he could help her. The only way.

The five doors of the second floor were all closed. He'd only been up there a few times, usually to help with Carrie. The door at one end was the bathroom, he knew that much. The other three were bedrooms back then, the small door to his immediate right a storage and linen closet. Going into each one might be considered snooping, but she was the one who'd sent him up here blind. He wasn't about to feel bad about what he found.

The first room was exactly what he remembered. Directly across from the stairs, it had been Carrie's. He'd expected Whitney to have changed it, but apart from the obvious dusting, nothing had altered. Carrie's hospital bed, neatly made with a well-worn quilt he remembered from childhood, still dominated the small space. An old pine dresser filled the corner across from it, decorated with at least a dozen glassless frames. Each one looked homemade, padded with fabric and lace. He recognized himself in more than a few, in snapshots with Whitney and the wallet size picture of his boot camp graduation.

A glance around the room and he saw more pictures, frames on every surface, on every wall. All of them memories Whitney had tried to keep in her mother's mind. It was a battle Whit never had a chance of winning, but she'd fought with every part of her being. It was the way she was made—a woman who gave her all, no matter how much it hurt.

The memory of her kiss hit him again, so viscerally he sucked in a breath. Her passion had been the same way. Nothing held back. Nothing hidden. It should have humbled him—that she could still do that after all she'd been through. Instead, guilt ate at him.

He couldn't.

He kept himself insulated. Separate, locking his emotions behind a wall of ice so thick they would never get out. He shored that wall up daily. The only one who'd ever breached it, burned it down without even trying, was her. Not even Shana ever got as deep as Whitney did.

So. Fucking. Dangerous.

Whitney scared the shit out of him…but he couldn't stay away from her. Sure as shit couldn't leave her in *this* situation. He couldn't give himself the physical distance he needed, had no idea how he could ignore the pull she had on him. But he would figure out how. Figure a way through all of it.

Which would have been easier if the next door wasn't Alison's room.

Chapter Eight

What. The. Hell.

The space was both a disaster and a showroom. The walls weren't so much painted as attacked. In every direction, color spattered. Black, white, blue, purple, and a disturbing amount of red. Not even the ceiling was spared. No frames, no posters. Just color thrown violently. Without pattern or form of any kind on most of the walls, the layers of splashed paint felt like screams coming from every direction. Something else had been thrown too, leaving gaping holes in the drywall. Big, small, nicks, dents, wide-open gashes with chunks dangling by a shred. As if the walls had been battered regularly.

The bed, a twin pushed to one side of the room, was made with military precision. White sheets, stark against a gray blanket. Pairs of shoes, lined up as if by a ruler, stood sentinel underneath. A narrow bookshelf and a drafting table took up the space by the door, the books inside arranged by uniform heights, though the bindings looked to be falling off. The table was blisteringly white, obviously scrubbed with bleach, and the deep blue carpet was equally clean. No clothes left out, no mess anywhere. Perfect order in a sphere of disaster.

The step near the top of the staircase creaked, giving away that he was about to be interrupted, but Rick didn't bother to hurry out. Whitney already knew where he was and he was going to hear about the snooping no matter what.

"You have always been the nosiest man alive, you know that?"

Not even remotely. That title fell on his father, who'd become a doctor so he could get all the good gossip straight from the horse's mouth.

"As soon as I heard the boots stop clomping, I knew you were in here. You can never restrain yourself from scoping out the enemy."

It *was* his job in the Marines.

"Impressive, don't you think?"

"The paint or the mounting terror?" He shifted in time to catch her rolling her eyes in the doorway.

"Alison has some problems—"

"Alison has a *psychosis*."

"Who here doesn't?"

He hated how much of a point she had. "You don't think it's odd she has a Rorschach test on her bedroom walls?"

"Actually," she leaned against the lintel, giving him a surprisingly successful arch look. She pointed at the wall behind him. "*I* did that one."

There wasn't any point in looking. "Yeah, I figured that out already."

"No, you didn't."

"It looks like a flower."

"It does no—" She turned her head, scrunching her whole face as realization hit. "Oh my God, it *is* a flower."

He gestured to the remaining three surfaces around them. "All I'm saying is that I know a guy at Pendleton who'd love to get his hands on her."

"Psychiatrist?"

"MP."

Her left eye squinted. "Don't make me call Katrina. Again."

Cade's wife, a former child delinquent herself, loved to rub his face in his old preconceptions about her. He'd survived worse than her good-natured ass kickings. "How can she be that messed up in her head and *that*," he pointed to the extreme order of her things around her bed, "restrained out here?"

"Because she's been through more than you know." The smile faded completely from Whitney's soft voice. "Vera… I'm still not sure what happened there. She started running away and acting completely out of control after she turned thirteen. After Aunt Kelly died, it just got so much worse. She wasn't ready to be a mother, dragging Alison everywhere she went, leaving her God knows where I don't know how many times. Alison still refuses to talk about it. But if you think repeated abandonment as well as any physical and emotional abuse she endured before she came to me didn't create a complicated psyche, I'm not the naïve one in the room, am I?"

Shit. "I don't trust her."

Whitney snorted. "God no. No one should trust her.

She's spent half her life pickpocketing and almost all of it lying to get what she wanted." His surprise must have shown because he got her smile back, this time a smug one. "You thought I didn't know that?"

"To be honest, no."

"I'm not a complete idiot, you know. And I'm not as sweet and innocent as you like to think, either."

The message there was clear, but it wasn't a gauntlet he could pick up.

"No one can live like that so long and just stop on a dime because their situation changed. When she first came here, she scared the crap out of me. She was angry and violent, sneaky and rude."

Rick considered Alison's near expulsion from school for fighting, her open hostility toward anyone in a position of authority, and the various holes around the room. "That's changed how, exactly?"

"She's settled down so much, Rick. I wish you could see it."

"I see that she's showing you what you want to see." For the first time in her life, Alison had someone stable, someone who cared about her enough to stay no matter what. It was why he couldn't let go of Whitney, either. Unfortunately, being able to relate to Alison had him snarling as he started out of the bedroom. "She gets out of hand in the slightest, you call me."

"If she gets out of hand, I'll handle it the same way I always do."

"Which is?" He pulled the door closed, making sure it fully engaged, exactly the way he found it. Just in case Alison was the paranoid type.

Whitney's laugh trilled over his senses, a salve without even trying. "I hide, like any other sane person. She wears herself out eventually." She kept walking down the hall to- ward the final door, oblivious she'd left him behind. It was only when she got close, her laughter dropping abruptly, that she stopped, hand extended tentatively. When it started to shake, she snatched it back.

"You go on in," she murmured, long seconds later. It was clear she knew he'd seen. "I don't go in there much. You'll have to excuse the dust."

"Whitney." He wanted to console her. Soothe away the shame coming off her tight shoulders and hands clenched to her belly. Tell her it would all be okay, that she didn't have to explain her fear. But it all bottled so tight in his chest he was choked by it and like always, all he could get out was her name. It wasn't enough. It was never enough. This time, watching her stare at the door the way one would contem- plate the gates of Hell, it didn't even seem to reach her. Her gaze remained locked on the door, like a spell she couldn't break.

Carefully, he stepped behind her, wincing when she jumped at the feel of his hand on her shoulder, spinning to slap him away. Just like in the bakery…

She shook her head, eyes closed tight, her body tight against the wall. Away from him. "I can't—"

"You don't have to." He didn't need the explanation, not when it hurt her like this.

"What happened in there, it's not what you think." Such a soft whisper, but it made him bleed all the same. She kept her eyes closed, her face so pale he thought she'd be sick any moment. Her entire body trembled but he was afraid to touch her again. "I made my choices that night, just like they did."

They? How he didn't stagger, he didn't know. One word and he thought he'd fallen to his knees.

"I locked Alison and my mother in her room, told her to play Mom's music as loud as she could. I hoped to God they wouldn't hear…" She took a long, rasping breath. "The point is, I walked in there on my own. That's why I never told you. Why I never meant to tell you anything about it. I'm not a victim for you to save or avenge. A fool, yes, but not a victim." She lifted her lashes, her eyes gleaming with unshed tears and unvarnished determination. "I will never forgive you if you treat me like one."

He knew a vow when he heard one. She needed his acceptance on this and damn if he would let her believe for a second she didn't have it. "Yes ma'am."

Relief softened the strain on her features before she cleared her throat delicately and stepped away from the wall. "The dresser by the window. Top drawer, back left corner. It'll tell you whatever you need to know."

Cupping her face with one hand when she would have passed him, he tilted her chin to get her to look him in the eye. "I don't need a gun to tell me you didn't do this. I don't need anything to tell me the kind of woman you are. I know, Whitney. Nothing that's happened to you—to either of us—will ever change that."

She stared up at him, her cool touch holding his hand tighter to her face, her tears finally overflowing to scald his skin. "Would you believe me if I said the same thing to you?"

He thought about saying no. With anyone else, it would have been automatic. Not her. She'd accepted his darkness, his nightmares, a long time ago. Never once expected his past to leave him simply because he was home. Never told him he had no right to his guilt. Never tried to absolve him of it. He could do the same for her…and burn down anyone who told her different. "Absolutely."

Her smile blinded him, so much so he never saw her kiss coming. Hard and fast, she pushed past him before he could do more than brush his fingers over the fabric of her dress in an effort to hold on. She disappeared, leaving him a task that had become infinitely more distasteful than before.

Refusing to let himself think any more, he entered the room. It shouldn't have been so innocuous. A simple bedroom, full of light and oak furniture. The bed made neatly with another quilt, this one all squares cut from floral pink fabric. Stupid, really, but he'd expected a preserved crime scene, with broken and discarded items strewn every which way. He'd also expected dust, as Whitney had warned, but the room was as immaculate as the rest of the house. Every frame gleamed, each surface polished. Intensely feminine, he could sense the warmth of her from the faded porcelain figurines to the blue and beige striped wallpaper and frilly pillows. Even the clothes in the open closet were straightened, the shoes on the floor in perfect rows…

Alison. She must have done this, carefully maintaining this room Whitney couldn't begin to enter. Couldn't even look into it. But if she ever did, Alison had made sure the nightmare wasn't there to slap her in the face. Forensically, he knew he should be horrified, but Whitney occupied that singular part of him that still operated emotionally and all he could feel was grateful.

Goddammit, now he was going to have to cut the girl

some slack. Probably even thank her. Shit, that would go down like a mouthful of rusty nails.

Still gritting his teeth, he put on his gloves and stalked to the tallboy dresser. True to her word, the satin-finished nickel-plated Bersa Thunder 22 was sitting in the back of the drawer, still in its leather muzzle. He lifted it, carefully pulling it from the drawer…completely unprepared for the filmy lace bra clinging to the hammer.

The whole thing was so epically *Whitney* he finally sighed, tension leeching out of him. If she were there, she'd be smiling again. Or laughing at him. Probably the only time he'd let her get away with it. He could just hear his father teasing him, too. *Finally got into Whitney's drawers, huh? Only took you thirty years…* Against his will, he smiled as he extracted the undergarment and dropped the gun into the evidence bag.

This was as close as he could see himself getting to her undergarments again. He couldn't ignore what had come out today. The things she'd hinted at, what she had already been through. Shit, the things she was still going through. She thought she could just shut it all out, pretend it wasn't still affecting her, but she was lying to herself. Her terror when he'd touched her shoulder—he could handle most anything but her looking at him with fear in her eyes. If he somehow pushed her into a flashback, the way he clearly almost did… No. *Fuck* no.

Hunger or not, he wasn't going to do that to her. He couldn't let her talk him into it, either. They absolutely could not cross that line. Right now, she was only a minor suspect in Cade's eyes, but that would change. The connection to Dewar had to be divulged and he could not be seen as a risk to the investigation or he'd lose the right to know what was happening. Her status wouldn't keep him away from her, though it should. No, her *secret* was the reason he would keep clear. Keep his hands to himself.

What had happened that morning wouldn't happen again. They'd go back to what they used to be. He'd do his job—*just* his job—to get her out of this mess. Ballistics would rule her weapon out and she'd be clear of suspicion. No one would be able to accuse her of jack shit. Done.

Then maybe, just maybe, they could get out of this thing without him ruining the only relationship in his life untainted by his mistakes. Maybe they could forget what it had been like to touch each other as people without scars. People who could still feel normal. Feel at all.

The only problem was, he had no idea where that would leave either of them.

• • •

Rick's house lay nestled in a copse of oak trees, surrounded on three sides by winding branches, each one as thick as her waist. Even in the brightest light of day, the broad one-storey building remained shrouded in shadows and utterly impregnable. It was perfect for him.

She didn't come out here often, since the property was well away from everyone and everything, offering few excuses to happen by. By design, she was sure. He couldn't have made his position clearer if he had painted the building black and written "Go Away" in day-glo orange on the front door.

But here she was, anyway. In her car, in the dark, trying

to convince herself to go inside. He'd let her in if she got herself up there. She knew what would happen if she did. What she was there to *make* happen. What she *needed* to make happen.

Don't make me come after you.

Fighting words she'd meant at the time. They weren't so easy to back up in the cold breeze of night, something he was clearly counting on. When the hours passed after he left her house without a word, she knew it had come down to this. No matter what she said, how happy or willing she was, he was backing off and making decisions for them both again. If she was going to change anything, she would have to run him to ground and this time, she couldn't let anything get in the way. Not his sense of valor, not her own terror that she was about to start something she wouldn't be able to finish. It was time for *her* to make some of the decisions.

At first, she'd gone about her strategy in as detached a way as possible. Alison had come home after school, thankfully preoccupied with her current art project. She'd been surprised when Whitney had said she was going out, but she hadn't questioned the money for pizza Whitney gave her or the plans she'd claimed to have. God bless Katrina and her standing invitation to the bar. In the end, Alison had been thrilled to have the house to herself for a few hours. Precious short hours to Whitney, but here she was, still wasting minutes counting the beige slats on Rick's front porch. Gripping the steering wheel like a lifeline, she was using any distraction she could find to put off making the most important choice of her life. Go in or leave. Change everything, either way.

She wanted to bang her head on the steering wheel.

How did he do this all the time?

She wasn't stupid. His lights were on, so she knew he was home. Which meant *he* knew she was sitting in her car like an idiot in front of his house. Only a moron would think he wasn't aware of everything that happened within five hundred yards of his personal fortress. More likely a mile.

But neither of them were moving.

If she drove away, he'd take it as agreement that they shouldn't take the next step in their relationship and disappear. Worse, he'd pretend nothing had happened and make sure nothing ever *would* happen. Truthfully, he might disappear no matter what she did. Which made taking the risk an obvious choice—she had nothing to lose. Except her self-respect. But really, how much of that did she have left, anyway?

The laugh at least got her to loosen her hold on the steering wheel and think. Could she really spend the rest of her life wondering if they could have had a chance?

No. She had enough regrets. She'd be damned before he became one. Grabbing her purse, she jumped out of the car, moving forward on pure nerve. Which helped immensely when his front door opened just as she lifted her hand to knock.

He was still in his uniform, the top button of his shirt undone, a beer hanging from his long-fingered hand. Thunder and lightning on that handsome face as he glowered down at her. "No, Whitney."

"Yes, Rick." She pushed past him into the house, dumping her purse next to the coat rack and kicking off her flats. Her coat came off next, falling off the hook she tried to hang it on. She ignored it.

"Damn it, we can't be— What the hell are you doing?" he demanded when her numb fingers started in on the row of buttons running from the neckline of her dress.

"Stripping. You might want to close the door. You never know when someone with a death wish might come driving by." The first button on the sweetheart collar finally gave. She slipped down to the next one, which at least got him to kick the door shut and slam the beer on the small lamp table next to his couch.

"We are not doing this."

Maybe she was getting a little hysterical, but the commanding tone of his voice almost made her laugh wildly. The poor man sounded a tad bit desperate. "Sure we are. We take off our clothes, get into your bed and nature takes its course. I even brought condoms. You still sleep in that back bedroom?" Three buttons down, she headed for the hallway next to the kitchen.

She spun in place instead, his hand hooked around her elbow. Her dress was gaping open now and she could feel the hot sweep of his gaze across the tops of her breasts before darting up to her face again. A telltale flush covered his cheeks. Good God, she'd made him blush! World-hardened, pseudo-robotic, badass Rick Trelane, blushing at the sight of her everyday ordinary boobs.

Look at that, maybe I am *a sex goddess!*

Not really, but this plan suddenly didn't seem so impossible. Modesty melted away completely when his gaze slipped again, his mouth tightening, as if he couldn't help himself. So, while he was busy tracing the swells above her demi-cups, she stepped closer and reached for his buttons.

His hand wrapped around her wrist to stop her, a move

she knew he intended to be intimidating, except his thumb rubbed small circles along her sensitive skin. And he was still staring at her breasts. "This is not a game."

"Says you." A yank from her free hand pulled both his uniform and the plain white undershirt from beneath his belt fast enough to surprise him. Taking advantage, she tugged her hand free and pulled out the other side.

"Goddamn it, Whitney!" He glared at her, batting her hands away. Lamely, in her opinion.

Unnerving this man might just be her new favorite pastime. She sidled close again and he didn't stop her. Not even when she slipped her hand under the loose shirts at his side, testing the hot, silken skin there. His muscles rippled under her touch. Sweet mercy, muscle was all she could feel. Unable to help herself, she kept going, traveling upward to his ribs, then swooping down the middle of him, her fingers grazing the tickling hairs leading to his navel and farther down—

His expletives this time should have singed her hair, his arms slapping around her and manacling her against his body. "Stop. Just stop."

"I don't want to."

"You don't want this."

This being the very aroused muscular body she was now pressed to from chest to toe? She lay her head back to look up at him, eyebrow raised.

The brilliant shade of his eyes glowed at her like hot embers when his gaze narrowed on her face. "I cannot give you what you're looking for. I keep telling you that."

"And what is it, exactly, that I'm looking for, Great Mind Reader Who Makes Decisions For Me Without My Permission?"

"More than just some mindless fuck on the floor," he snapped, still holding her tight, though she could see he wanted to shake her. "I'm not someone anyone turns to for comfort or kindness. For me, sex is physical only. An itch to be scratched. When it's over, I leave and I never look back. I won't use you like that, do you understand? So, stop pushing me. We'll both regret it if you do."

Her hands curled into the fabric of his shirt, gripping them so tight he had to feel the pull. She didn't care. She couldn't give in. She wouldn't fold under his will, not when it was this important. "Then let me use you."

His confusion was obvious, but it didn't seem to change his plan to keep her bound. So close, there was nowhere else to look but at his face. She ran her tongue over suddenly dry lips, bravado failing her when she needed it the most. She should have expected this. With him, the truth was almost always the only option. Even if it hurt—and God knew, it would hurt—it was all she had to give him.

"I have wanted you for as long as I've known what wanting was. As long as it was all in my head, it never mattered. I never thought anything might ever happen between us. But that all changed when you kissed me. For the first time in my life, my imagination couldn't begin to compete."

If he'd argued with her, it would have broken her heart. Instead, all he did was tug her closer, her face to his chest, so his hold was more a hug, his chin resting atop her head. She closed her eyes, breathing him in deep before she took that final step, giving him a truth that had haunted her for so long, she'd thought it was a permanent part of her. "I never thought I could feel like that again. When you touched me, all I felt, all I could think of was you. *Us.* I wasn't scared.

I wasn't frozen. I didn't feel filthy afterward. I was…happy. Terrified, but happy."

His heartbeat thudded against her ear. Strong and fast, almost as fast as hers.

"It's been so long since I wanted anyone. Since my body felt like it was mine to do with what I wanted. Maybe it's because my feelings for you are older, stronger than what happened. Or maybe it's because I'm ready to try to move forward. I don't know and analyzing it just makes me worry that I'll ruin it. All I know is that I'm safe with you. I feel *good* with you. And I think you feel the same with me. Maybe that scares you. Maybe it should. But I'm not willing to walk away from it, from you, just because you tell me to."

The rough stubble of his jaw stroked the side of her face, the strength of his arms softening until she could finally hold him, too. Did he know he was doing it? Giving comfort, maybe even receiving it.

She melted into him, rubbing cheeks she only just realized were wet, into his shirt. "I don't want *him* to be the last man to touch me. No matter what happens with us afterward, I want it to be you."

He sighed against her hair, a sound that could have come from his toes. "You don't fight fair."

She smiled, a wet kind of laugh escaping her while she rubbed her hands up and down his back. It felt so good to be held like this. If he still pushed her out the door, the trip would still have been worth it. "That's what I keep telling you. I don't want to fight at all. I want a memory for both of us. Something good. Is that really so much to ask?"

Of course it was. She knew it was. But she needed him. More than that, she knew he needed her just as much, maybe more. That thought gave her the courage to rise up on her toes and fit her lips to his. He held back, not pushing her away, but definitely not giving in. Frustration, dismay, welled through her. She couldn't let this go. "*Please.*"

He gasped against her lips, his entire body tightening like a bowstring being yanked.

She lifted herself higher, pulling back only enough to whisper words she hoped he couldn't ignore. "I need you, Rick. I need you so much…"

He held out for a beat, two, but then he groaned, turning them so her back was against the wall. They hit it with a slam, his swearing the oddest thing to find sexy. Like the sound of a dam breaking, she thought distantly, the one sided kiss suddenly erupting into something that stole her breath completely.

He swept into her, a firestorm of need, demanding, pulling, inundating her senses. His taste, a dark, exotic flavor, his presence becoming the absolute center of her world. His big hands cupped her behind, lifting her high against him. Her legs clamped onto him of their own accord, her hands finding purchase around his neck. It should have been overwhelming, especially when he began walking with her, but relief at his acceptance was almost as strong a drug as his kiss. Only one word echoed in her mind as he carried her down the hall.

More.

Chapter Nine

Deep kisses.

Hard.

Wet.

Drugging.

Whitney had both hands buried in Rick's hair, a fantasy all its own. The thick masses feathered between her fingers, warm and almost as alive as the man holding her. Heat from his body, the texture of his lips sliding over hers, even his hands supporting her while he walked them down the hall. She tried to memorize every sensation, every moment, failing fantastically because he was kissing her and scrambling her brain more with every lick and rumbled murmur of approval.

Softness under her knees. His bed. He slid back on it, with her still straddling him, until his back met the headboard. She reached for the top edge of it, steadying herself over him. It should have been awkward, her most sensitive flesh pressing down on his thick erection, still bound beneath his uniform pants. Someday, she knew she'd find the whole thing laughable and insane, but right now, she was concentrating on the feel of his teeth nibbling down the column of her neck. Rough padded fingers traced the open edges of her dress collar, tugging them past her shoulders. He helped her slip her arms from the dress, the material falling down around her waist in a flutter that matched her racing heartbeat.

"So, while you're using me," he murmured, gravelly voice tickling her neck. Deeper than usual. Rough. "Do I get to look at you?"

"Hmm?" Gentle strokes over the slopes of her breasts, light as a whisper. The backs of his knuckles?

"I want to see you, Whitney. Can I turn on the light?"

Oh, the light. Light would be good...

"Will I get to see you too?" She'd only waited her entire life for this moment, might as well ask for what she wanted.

"Not sure that's a good idea."

Oh God, his whole hand slid up her chest to curl around her nape and pull her closer to his still wandering mouth. His breath, his voice, the lulling circles he was drawing on the small of her back... She was mesmerized. "I think it's a great idea."

"Scars. You don't need to see those."

She pulled back a little, glaring at him despite the darkness. Purposely slow, she reached out to the lamp she remembered from the times she'd brought him food during his recovery. The small plastic knob under the cylindrical shade clicked, a soft yellow glow melding the shadows around them into intimate shades of gray. She found him watching her just as intently in the light. "Will you think less of me for *my* scars?"

"That's not even a question."

"Sure it is." She brushed her fingers over the pale line on her clavicle. "Remember when I fell out of the tree we were climbing when we were ten?" The rock she'd landed on had cut the skin and cracked the bone. When he nodded, she stroked the strap of her bra off her shoulder, his eyes tracking the movement the way he would a target. How did she never know he was so interested in her breasts?

"What about my freckles?" She used her left hand to trail over her neck and down to her breastbone. "Do those bother you?"

"You know they don't." His eyes glinted, already trained on the second strap, waiting with fine impatience for her to move it down.

She did, painstakingly slow. "I'm pretty pale. Women like me don't tan very well." She sat back, reaching her arms behind herself, waiting for his response.

His expression inscrutable, he cupped her jaw, his thumb moving back and forth over her bottom lip. "There *are* no other women like you."

"Oh, that's a very good answer." One that made it very easy to undo the hooks at her back. Her bra fell away, leaving her completely vulnerable to him. But he didn't look down, instead keeping his gaze locked on hers while she peeled the straps off her wrists and tossed the undergarment away.

"It's the only answer."

Startled, she could only blink at his gruff response. Then she sighed. This moment, right this second, was why she loved him. Had always loved him. His hunger was plain on his face, the sleepy seduction in his eyes, that tint of a flush over his cheekbones she vowed then and there never to tell him about. She could feel his body's reaction beneath her, his insistent erection impossible to ignore, but he was never the kind of man to put his own desires first. He was protecting her, proving to her that she was safe even now that she was bared. That she mattered to him as more than a body.

He'd said he couldn't do that. Couldn't give her the emotional connection she wanted from him. But he was. Not by coddling her. Not with flowery words that would have sounded like lies. By simply accepting her, looking in her eyes and not letting her feel like she was just a body to him, something worthless and empty.

His hands slowly trailed down her arms, landing on her waist again. Inch by inch, he traced his way up her rib cage. Giving her plenty of time to back away, watching her face for any sign of rejection, he finally cupped her breasts. She shivered, leaning into his hands and moaning when his thumbs skated over the peach tinted tips. She arched, wanting more, hips twitching with each swirl of his thumbs. Pleasure struck like lightning when he leaned forward to take one in his mouth. And when the edge of his teeth clasped down on her nipple, she couldn't begin to hold back a cry of surprise. Of excitement.

Eyes trained on hers, he shifted to the other breast. He slid the tip back and forth between his lips, as if he had all the time in the world to play with her body. All the while, his hands pet her, molding and plumping her flesh while his tongue flicked out to drive her insane. The more he teased, suckling at her until she quaked, then moving that hot, dangerous mouth up her chest, back to her throat where he could deliver the same maddening treatment to her pulse, the more she craved doing the same to him.

"This needs to come off," she managed to mutter, tugging at his uniform shirt.

He growled a dissent, not stopping what he was doing in the slightest. "Shhh. I'm busy."

God, why hadn't she realized he'd be even more provoking in bed than out of it? Well, two could play that game. "If you don't take this off, I won't tell you what I'm not wearing under my dress."

That made him hesitate, but only for a second. His hand quickly smoothed down and around her back, slipping under the gathered fabric of her dress to the flesh of her bare bottom. She gasped as he squeezed, a guttural sound of appreciation rumbling out of his chest. He continued to stroke there, lifting her forward, making her more aware of her disconcerting wetness increasing by the second. She couldn't remember being this aroused in her life, and they'd only just gotten started. But here she was, living out a fantasy where Rick's slightly roughened fingertips were touching her intimately. Seeking…*finding*…her slick folds. Sweet God…

"I'm pretty sure not wearing panties counts as cheating in this game of yours."

She shook her head, her eyes fluttering shut as those magical fingers pet her again, sliding slowly over her labia. More circles, small, gently probing, somehow soothing the ache in her and stoking it up at the same time. "A girl has the right to use everything she's got."

"Everything *you've* got might kill me." He found her opening, sinking the tip of his finger inside. She shuddered, unconsciously pushing onto it, still wanting more, but he pulled back with a scowl. "You're determined to rush me, too?"

"Next time, you can go as slow as you like." Not now, not when she'd waited so long. Tonight, she needed to feel her way through, to be overwhelmed in the best way. "I warned you not to make me come after you. Now you've got to deal with it however I see fit."

How she had the nerve to take control, she didn't know, but she attributed it to the same thread of desperation that made her yank his shirt open, dragging it over his shoulders where it trapped his arms in place. "Skin, Trelane. Now."

Maybe he understood. Maybe he was in the same needy state as she was, but he finally helped her peel the clothes off his torso, bearing all that golden skin and rippling muscle. Tempted to whistle, she settled for licking her lips in anticipation.

He hadn't lied about the marks she'd find. The tattoo over his left pectoral—the Marine's eagle, globe, and anchor—was marred by a jagged line, as if someone had tried to cut his heart right out. She held in the urge to stroke it, to ask what had happened. This wasn't the time. He was trusting her not to. She refused to betray him, no matter how much she wished she could remove the hurt. It wasn't the only scar to worry over. Round circle scars, different sizes, scattered in different places. Four of them that she could see without searching. Bullet wounds, she supposed, knowing his time overseas had been brutal. A palm-length surgical line bisected his belly, starting just below his ribs, faint beneath the coarser brown hair sprinkling down his chest. A world of pain, something he considered simply a part of himself.

Next time, she promised herself, hoping there would be one. Next time, she would kiss each one. For now, she concentrated on learning the textures and planes of his body. Each muscle, hot and firm to her touch. She stayed alert for any reaction from him, trying to see what pleased him. It wasn't easy, since the freedom to stroke him was almost as intoxicating as his hands on her. He said nothing, letting her run her palms over him while he watched her through slitted lids. A tiger, content in his cage for the time being. Letting her decide where this was going.

She leaned down, grazing her lips over his. Still passive, he let her pull back. The next kiss, he opened for the tentative lick she gave his bottom lip, allowing her another. And another, and another. Each one longer than the last. His hands settled on her thigh, gentling her until they found their way up to her hips. By then, he was guiding her fraught little movements on his lap into a steady rocking motion against him.

Inside, a small part of her trembled, near panic. Like a faint vibration only she could hear, growing louder and louder within her. Waiting for the first sign of danger, ready to rip her out of pleasure's grasp. For all that she tried to tune it out, rush past it, it was his slow, soothing movements that drowned it out. Gently drawing her deeper and deeper into a slow erotic haze. His hands never stopped moving, gliding over her breasts, her back, her hips and ass before starting all over again. His mouth made a trail of fire back and forth from one nipple to the other. The demanding jut of his cock pressed temptingly against her sex, an inexorable reminder of what was to come. Curiosity and desire warred constantly with trepidation, but he never let her go too fast.

So, it wasn't any wonder how she missed it at first. The restraint he was using. His careful, slowly paced breaths. The tremor in his fingertips.

He wasn't with her.

He was still thinking. Still cautious. Watching her every reaction the way he would one of those bombs she knew he made overseas. That wasn't what she wanted. Or what she was going to let him get away with.

Her hands itched to explore him, to bring him into the same spell he was weaving around her. She inched her fingers downward, easing her nails over his flat nipples, gasping as he bucked beneath her. Definitely a spot to remember…

Washboard abs were the next challenge. Deceptively smooth, his muscles had almost no give, jumping from time to time as she traced his midline. Springy brown hair tickled her fingertips until the trail disappeared beneath the heavy polyester of his uniform pants. Gathering her courage once again, she reached for his waistband, trying to undo the most daunting button so far.

He broke the kiss, hissing out a breath as she undid the button flap. When she began to tug on the zipper, he shackled her wrist, cupping the back of her neck with the other hand and pulling her ear to his mouth. "Last chance, Whit. Be sure."

She shook, equal parts desire and fear pumping through her blood. Not of him, not even of this moment. Of losing this—herself—to the terror underlying every second of it. She refused to let any more of her choices be taken from her. *Refused*.

"I've never been more sure of anything in my life." *I love you…* Words she could never say, but she hoped he felt. She hoped they reached the parts of him he so firmly believed were gone. "I want to feel you inside me. I want to feel you all over every part of me. So when I close my eyes, there's only you."

And when he closed his, she wanted to be the only one he saw. The one he dreamed about. As fantasies went, she knew it was impossible, but she wanted it so badly she let herself hope. After all, she never imagined *this* was possible, either.

His jaw flexed, his hold on her nape almost shaking. "I'm trying to be gentle with you. Trying to take care of you, but you're making it fucking impossible to keep control."

She couldn't have held back her smile if she tried. Instead, she pressed it to the side of his face, kissing his cheek and rubbing his ever present stubble against her lips. "Isn't the whole point to lose control?"

She ran the edge of her teeth over his earlobe, licking the sting away with the tip of her tongue. She wanted to do the same to the column of his throat. Wanted to mark him, so everyone would know he was hers, if only for the night. Then she realized… She could. He'd given her that right. She bent lower, opening her mouth over his skin. Closing her eyes, she tasted the salt of him, savored it. Then she began to suck.

All of a sudden, she was on her back, surrounded by him. His arms on either side of her, crowding her close, his tongue exploring her mouth with a thoroughness that left her breathless, his hips grinding into hers, the thick thrust of him inescapable now.

The tiger had burst free.

Maybe in both of them. It felt so good to wrap her legs around him, make him thrust harder. It wasn't deep enough, satisfaction frustratingly far away. She arched up into his chest, her hands gripping his upper arms, the vague recognition of a scar behind his left bicep. She almost questioned it, but he tore himself from her mouth just far enough to whisper, "Stop me, Whit. I'll never forgive myself if I hurt you."

"There's nothing to forgive." She held his face with both hands, feeling him shuddering to hold back from her still. "There never has been."

"I just don't want you to look at me like…" *Them*. The word he didn't want to say. Didn't want to bring into this room, though they both knew the memories were there nonetheless. Wariness clouded his eyes, along with the shadows of pain he couldn't seem to let go of.

She would take the pain from him if she could. If he'd let her, but she knew he wouldn't. So, she'd give what he did allow. Touch. Acceptance. Love, whether he knew it or not. She'd give him everything and hope it was enough to reach him.

For now, the reassurance he needed was something she knew how to offer. "That won't happen. I know *you're* the one touching me." She kissed him gently, making sure he was looking in her eyes when she said, "Lose control. Just make sure to take me with you."

He still seemed skeptical, though his body hadn't lost any of its tension. Or, from what she could feel against her thigh, his interest. So stubborn.

"Maybe I'll take *you* with *me*," she challenged, stealing another kiss. The next landed on his cheek. She tightened her legs around him, lifting her hips, smiling when he rumbled into her neck. Teasing movements, until his hands grasped her hips, guiding her once more.

"So. Fucking. Dangerous," he growled, bucking against

her again, swallowing her surprised cry with another of his devouring kisses.

She writhed beneath him, rubbing as much of her skin against him as she could, reveling in him. Her entire body was quivering now. Suddenly, his hand was there again, reaching between them, parting her folds. Testing her. Groaning when he felt exactly how ready she was. A firm finger dipping into her again, caressing within, while his thumb circled her clitoris. Not nearly as careful this time, but far more devastating to her equilibrium. Pleasure turned her entire body to honey, and she felt as if she were sinking. Sinking into the moment, into sensation, into the delicious feel of him actually making love to her.

"Next time," he murmured, looking down at her, not stopping the slow stirring he was doing with his fingers. "I get to taste you."

"God, yes." Her mind reeled at that mental picture. The moist heat of his mouth drew at her nipple, firing her imagination nearly enough to throw her into oblivion.

"Not yet, Whit. You promised to take me with you, remember?" He rose up on his haunches, eyeing her in her complete disarray as if she were an elaborate dessert he had every intention of consuming, one bite at a time. He turned to reach for something in his bedstand. The sound of foil tearing told her what it was. Then he was ripping at his zipper, leaning back, freeing himself from his clothes. She watched, unabashed, as he fit the latex over the wide head of his sex, fisting himself and rolling it down the shaft.

Next time she would do it, she decided, the flutter of excitement in her belly doubling. He reached out to her and she took his hand, letting him pull her to her knees. Her dress fluttered down her legs and she left it behind, following as he directed her into straddling him once more. He leaned back against the headboard, looking up at her while gathering her close. Completely nude, her belly against his chest, his hand fitting possessively over her breast while his arm wrapped around the small of her back.

"You lead," he said, his hand gliding down her flank and back up. He smoothed over her as if she were silk. As if he'd never felt anything so fine…

She stared down into his eyes, so vivid, so arresting, and had the strangest sense of empowerment. Maybe not so strange, her sexuality something she had never given much thought to. But right now, time stopped while he waited for her to move, to accept him, and there was no denying the thrill of having him at her mercy. Finally, finally, she relaxed completely into his hold, letting go the breath she didn't know she'd been holding.

Only then did he move. He took her hands, one at a time, and placed them on his shoulders. "It's just us. And we have all the time in the world. Nothing else matters."

No pressure. No judgment. Even if she wanted to stop right now. She nodded, the shaking vibration rising up in her again, trying to take control. She tamped it down, determined not to give in. They'd earned this, damn it.

She nodded again, allowing herself to sink carefully downward. His palm slid to her hip, guiding her over him. The other wrapped tight around his shaft, an erotic sight she couldn't tear her gaze from. Aiming himself to her aching core. And she was aching, needing to be filled.

Still, it took all her bravery, when the broad shape of him first nudged her. She gasped, holding herself still while he stroked slowly, so slowly, letting her get used to the intrusion. Their gazes locking, she sank the tiniest bit downward, capturing him within her. She didn't dare breathe, taking him in a little deeper.

Inch by desperate inch, her body accepted his possession. Until she finally had all of him, so full she could barely draw in the next breath. The fear fell back, settling ebb by ebb, at the lack of pain. Of terror. This experience was so delicate, so…lovely. There was no place for fear. She smiled at him, so ridiculously pleased with herself, with him, she wanted to throw her arms around him and laugh.

God love him, he smiled back. Encouraging. Proud, even. For a second, maybe less, she could see the boy she'd loved, still there in that mischievous grin. It made her feel young, hopeful in a way she'd forgotten.

Pure. That's what it was. Pure delight and joy at discovering something special together. Something just for the two of them.

It was a fraction of a second, a moment she'd never forget, and then it was washed away in the tide of need, her body demanding more. As, she realized, was his. He throbbed within her, starting an uproar all throughout. She jerked, surprised. He hissed, his hand tightening on her, urging her to do it again.

She rose up, sliding down his length again, turning her sigh into a delicious gasp. Again she lifted, her muscles clinging to him on the way up, the downward glide this time was better. Instinct began to take over, especially when he captured her nipple again, nibbling while he licked. He started to lead, his hands teaching her to roll the way he wanted.

Soon, all she could hear were her own sighs, his murmured

encouragement, and the roughening pace of their breathing. Her head fell back, arms crossed behind his head so he didn't stop sucking that spot on her neck. His thumb sought out her clit again and thought completely disappeared. Passion turned to an inferno. She moved desperately, wanting more, wanting everything. All he was. All he'd ever wanted to be. All she'd never been able to give. That she'd never received. It all blended into a maelstrom until the pressure of it snapped, shocking a cry from them both, leaving them shuddering in each other's arms.

And still he held her, his head against her heart. Did he hear it telling him she loved him? He didn't say and she didn't ask. But she took hope in the one thing she didn't have to ask him for.

He didn't let go.

Chapter Ten

She slept. Utterly trusting, completely relaxed, her ear pressed to his heart. He'd gotten rid of their tangle of clothing a while ago, tucking her along with him under his blankets. Without a word, she'd cuddled into him, sighing as she'd drifted off. The only sound in the house now was their breathing, soft and even. He found himself following hers, immersing himself in the quiet moment. In an odd way, it reminded him of sniper training. Laying in tall grass, the sun on his back, a breeze whispering past his face, his body in tune with his surroundings.

Peaceful.

She made him peaceful.

He frowned, not sure how he felt about that knowledge. His hand must have stuttered in petting her because she stirred, curling tighter to him. He went back to stroking, picking up the steady glide from her shoulder, down to the small of her back, and over the swell of her hip. Then all the way back up. She settled again, a puff of a sigh against his chest, and he exhaled the breath he'd been holding.

He wasn't ready for her to wake up. When she did, they'd have to talk. Have to analyze what they'd done and he'd have to admit he wasn't sure where to begin or what to do next. All he knew was she was turning his entire existence upside down.

The rules he'd written for himself didn't seem to apply anymore. She had him snapping them one after another without thought or regret. He had no idea how to handle that, especially now that everything was so much more complicated.

She'd been upgraded to an official suspect by the Sheriff's department. He'd gone round after round with Cade about it after admitting she could connect the two victims. Then, he'd stormed home to come up with some kind of plan to keep her safe. A plan he knew damn well she wouldn't participate in because *she* was still keeping her goddamn secrets. And why? Why couldn't she trust him with those when she trusted him with herself?

Why couldn't he *ask* her to?

He pushed out a breath. He didn't want to be angry right now. Didn't want to deal with any of the ugliness waiting outside the walls of his house. It would intrude sooner rather than later, anyway. All he wanted was for this moment to last a little longer. To not think about anything but how good she felt against him. To memorize the smoothness of her skin, savor the sweetness of her still in his mouth. Relax in the feel of her stretched from head to toe along his frame. To hold on to this quiet. This peace.

And no small dose of amazement.

Sweet little Whitney had walked into his house and seduced him. Derailed all his better judgment and probably his worse judgment while she was at it. *Let me use you.* All this time, he thought she had no ability to lie believably. He knew what being used felt like. That wasn't it. That was…

She'd been loving him. Every kiss, each touch. Even laced with demand, he could feel her trying to soothe him. Trying to take his pain and give him something beautiful. And she did. That was the amazing part. She'd taken the ravenous hunger in him and softened it to a tenderness no one in their right mind would believe possible from him. *He* still didn't believe it.

Then, of course, she redefined the meaning of fire for him. Leaving him confused about what he wanted, more confused about what was right, and beyond confused about what he could possibly say when she lifted those golden lashes and expected…what?

That was his biggest problem. What would she expect? That they would keep sleeping together? That this was the start of something more? It couldn't be. There was too much in the way. Not the least of which included that he might have to arrest her. For murder. Of the two men who had raped her. Which she wouldn't admit had happened. Next to that, her niece's desire to stab him in the eye with a fork wasn't as much of a concern, but even Alison had to be considered. As would the danger he posed to her heart. Her entire damn life. Tonight was probably the biggest mistake they'd ever made.

Except he was already starving for her again. Like a gnawing in his belly, a craving that bunched his muscles with every pass of his hand over her skin. The scent of her, of them, only made his appetite stronger. He was a match in a burning room, needing only a glimpse of her acceptance to go off.

Funny how all the logic in the world didn't stand a chance against that.

He ran his thumb over her plump bottom lip. Her face scrunched in response, making his chest ache. Not the bad kind, like when his kevlar took a hit. Something gentle, but somehow deeper. He did it again, curling his fingers to run his knuckles over her cheek. The ache grew deeper. So did his hunger.

Her lashes fluttered, finally opening the smallest amount. A throaty moan escaped her and a sultry smile curved her mouth. He wanted to taste it. Now.

"I was having the best dream," she murmured.

"Yeah? What about?" He traced the edge of her jaw.

"You were touching me."

"Mm hmm." His hand slipped into her hair. Possibly the softest texture he'd ever felt.

"I liked it." Husky voiced. Almost purring. "I liked it a lot." Her thick curls wrapped themselves around his fingers. Much like the woman herself. Stretching, her leg coursed up his flank, curling over his hip. Her back arched, pushing her breasts into him. It was like she was coming alive, swirling around him. Her lashes lifted completely, her gaze still sleepy, still hazy with passion. So fucking beautiful he wasn't sure he could breathe.

Her hand rose up, her fingers trailing up his chest to curve possessively around his neck, pulling him down for a kiss that scorched. Her tongue explored his mouth, unapologetically sexual. She moaned into him, her leg tightening at his waist. He couldn't get more of a resounding yes than that. He rolled fully over her, was quickly rewarded by both her hands in his hair. It took willpower he didn't know he had to pull back, breathing raggedly above her, to make sure she was awake enough to consent. She smiled, licking her lips. "Next time we fight, we're *so* doing it naked."

A rough bark of a laugh tore free and the look in her eyes turned to delight. "I love making you laugh."

"You're the only one who does." And at the damnedest times, too. Here he was, hard enough to break concrete, laughing.

"Then we're even, because you're the only one who makes me feel like this, too." She lifted up to steal another kiss, using that sneakiness he never saw coming. The same way he didn't expect the nip at his lips. "Don't stop."

She went back to kissing him, undulating her hips, gently twisting his brain into scrambled spaghetti while he blindly felt inside his bedside drawer. It took a ridiculous amount of time to find the damn condom, even more to fit it on without embarrassing himself when Whitney decided to "help." It was worth it, though, when he finally sank home inside her.

Her lashes fluttered again, her body clasping him so tightly he felt like a kid, not knowing if he'd be able to last for her. But then she looked up, their gazes locking. Holding him steady. Anchoring him.

He didn't know when they started to move. A slow rocking motion, dripping with pleasure. He came down to his elbows, fitting his forearms under her body. Gripping her shoulders, pulling her tighter to him with each slow thrust. She held on to his neck, not willing to let him get too far, lifting herself to take him deeper. He didn't think anymore, couldn't worry about the rights and wrongs of it. He could only move with her, feel her, give her what she needed. Take what she gave in return. Demand more, until both of them were panting. Until she was crying out, thighs clenching his waist, her body fisting and quivering so tight around him he lost sense of everything. Moving on instinct. On need. The wave of orgasm took him under so hard, so brutally, that everything turned white in his mind. There was only silence. Peace.

Whitney.

Her hands smoothing over his back. Her kisses on his face, his neck. Her whispers in his ears. Just Whitney. Just everything that mattered.

God. How was he going to give her up?

• • •

"This one?" Whitney traced her finger over the jagged line across Rick's pectoral. It was the third scar she'd asked about, stroking each one, placing a kiss in her own wake. She was laying on top of him now, her legs between his, free to touch wherever she wanted while he toyed with her hair. He kept running his fingers through the strands, letting her curls separate and come back together again once he let them go. Strangely soothing. Definitely intimate. She liked this. No, she loved it. Loved the quiet and the warmth and the closeness. Loved that he was letting her hold him, without any kind of argument or remorse. It might not last, but she wanted to enjoy every second she could steal.

"Hand to hand with an insurgent." Distracted. As if he didn't mind the questions when she knew damn well he normally did. But he wasn't being his normal, restrained self at the moment. The tiger in bed with her was sated now, she thought with a grin. Not quite sleepy, but that razored edge of tension had definitely tapered off.

His gaze shifted to watching her draw circles on his chest, then up to her face. That coolly burning gaze now studied her. Thinking. She knew that plotting expression. He was making decisions again. She was curious what he'd come up with this time, given the possessiveness of his hand on the small of her back. Holding her very much in place. It felt distinctly like he was going to keep it there forever.

She might be inclined to let him. "Why didn't they send you home for this?"

He frowned, finally starting to notice the conversation. "I had a few weeks' medical leave. It didn't incapacitate me."

"It would incapacitate *me.*" She raised her arm to show him the shiny discolored blotch on the inside of her forearm. "This is my only serious claim to fame. Got into a fight with an oven pan. As you can see, I didn't win. This was before those self-defense lessons you gave me, of course."

His cheeks creased, one of those faint grins that made her insides do a little flip. "Of course."

"I may have lost the fight, but I eventually won the war. That pan is in my garden now, I use it as a shelf for my herbs."

"That'll teach it."

"You're laughing at me." Exactly what she'd wanted.

"Well, when you consider that most of the things *I* fight end up dead…" That'd be funnier if he wasn't serious.

She blinked. Okay, try another tack. "So, how many times have you been shot?"

"Why? I'm still here." He seemed genuinely baffled that

she'd care.

Did he really not know her heart was in her throat every time his father was notified that he'd been hurt? Whenever she didn't get one of his incredibly brief letters from overseas? No, he probably never thought about it. He never seemed to think about how important he was to the ones who loved him. And telling him wouldn't help. "I'm taking a poll. Person with the most bullet wounds gets a cookie."

"With googly-eyes?" Ahh, now he was getting it.

"I might even be willing to trade up to a whole box of pralines."

His brows rose. She returned the look and he sighed, shaking his head and rolling his eyes. "You really were a bulldog in a past life, weren't you?"

"According to my mother, yes." There, another almost indulgent grin. "I'm just trying to find out all your secrets while you're too relaxed to argue."

"I'm never relaxed enough for that."

No kidding. She sighed, laying her head over the scar, listening to the deep, rhythmic beats of his heart. "You have to have somewhere to rest, Rick."

"Telling you about my scars doesn't put the past to rest. The past never rests."

"Maybe." She couldn't say her past ever fully left her alone. Her nightmares attested to that. "But that doesn't mean you have to carry it alone."

He remained quiet, his free hand back in her hair. Not angry quiet. Thinking quiet. Then, finally, "You carry yours alone."

She squinted an eye up at him. "I walked right into that, didn't I?"

His serious look was back. All that work, completely undone.

"I didn't have anyone to share it with."

"I've been here for the last four years." She knew that growl of growing irritation well.

"No, you were *present*. And you were saving everyone in town. Kind of a lot on your plate already. Besides, you weren't going to *share* my problems. You wanted to *solve* them for me."

"Isn't that what you're doing right now? Trying to fix me?"

"No."

"No?" Okay, he didn't believe that at all. Well, he didn't have to, she supposed.

"Sometimes it helps to have someone listen. To have them understand, even if they can't change what's happening."

"Now you sound like that therapist."

"The one you and Cade lied to so you could get discharged?"

"I never said I lied to him."

It was utterly satisfying to be the one with the disbelieving raised eyebrow.

He shrugged.

"I had no right to dump more of my problems on your lap back then." She'd wanted to, though. Wished all along that he would do the same, but it was an intimacy he didn't invite.

"And now?"

She smiled, laying her chin back on her hand. "I'll take your lead, I guess. Same as always."

He frowned. Hard. "You have *never* taken my lead. Not once in our whole lives."

"You were leading just fine a little while ago."

He opened his mouth to argue, catching himself at the last second and glaring instead.

"I know you, Rick. Well enough that I don't need to ask all those questions you find so annoying." People asking how he felt, what he thought, what he wanted when all three were pretty damn clear. "I knew where my limits were with you and I tried to respect them. I'm still trying to, which is why I'm not demanding answers. I'm offering an ear. One that won't judge you. The same as I'd ask from you, but only if you offered it."

Strangely, that reasonable explanation didn't seem to make him any happier.

"What?" she asked, perplexed at the growing thunder on his expression.

He shook his head, looking away. Well, that couldn't be good.

"What did I do now?"

"It's what you're not doing."

"Oh," she hadn't realized he'd changed the subject back to sex. "I thought you'd need more time but oka—" She shrieked a bit when he lifted her and rolled them simultaneously. His kiss quieted her to a deeply pleased moan. He didn't stop until she was clinging to his shoulders, melted in nearly every sense of the word.

"You never ask me for anything," he panted, gaze sharp enough to cut, his brows drawn together. "You give and you give, but you never ask. Do you know what an asshole it makes me, taking all the goddamn time?" He kissed her again, still rough, still frustrated, but she was slowly realizing—in the part of her brain somehow still able to think—that he wasn't angry at her. Her mind fought to stay clear, to follow this new direction, but he wasn't letting her. Finally, she had to push him up.

"Wait, you *want* me to make demands on you?"

"No, I…shit!" He said it so forcefully she giggled. And got glared at. "*This* is what I mean when I say you confuse me. *This* is what I was trying to avoid."

So…not sex. "You're going to have to spell it out for me, because I have no idea what you're talking about."

He closed his eyes again, forehead pressed to hers. She should have felt caged, wrapped tight in his hold, but it was oddly cherishing. He'd always been protective, but everything between them was suddenly new and old at the same time. Confusing and somehow so clear… *Ohhhh.*

"You care too much," she whispered, remembering all his warnings. He hadn't wanted to care about his sex partner, not beyond the act itself. He didn't know how to walk away from her like she didn't matter. She glanced up apologetically. "I just trampled all your relationship phobias, didn't I?"

He didn't open his eyes, but he did chuckle.

"Maybe we could…"

They opened now, beautifully bright and with that single-mindedness of his made painfully clear, making her next question so much harder to ask.

"If you can let me ask this without getting mad at me—" Though he did seem to kiss her when he was mad, so maybe that wasn't the worst idea. "Do you *want* this again or was tonight enough for you?" He'd seemed like he couldn't get enough of her, the way he'd stroked her awake and then made love to her like there was nothing else in the world that mattered. It would crush her if he turned her away now, but she had to ask. Had to know.

"No," he replied, his rough voice full of finality. Stronger than when he'd tried to deny her at the door, which nearly broke her heart. Until he curved his palm over her cheek. "Not nearly enough."

She dragged in a shaky breath, wishing she could hide the relieved wetness that stung her eyes. "Me, either. See, that wasn't…difficult." God help her, she'd almost said hard. "But you're still worried about something."

"You. I'm worried about you."

"Because I don't ask enough from you?"

"Among other things. But even if you did, I don't think I could give it to you." And he'd always be dreading the moment she asked for more than he could offer.

"Right," she said, deciding to keep that last thought to herself. "What with you being an emotional cripple and all. You're right, that could get bumpy." She pretended not to see his scowl. He really was good at all that glowering. She turned in his hold, spooning her back to his chest, holding onto the arm he'd had beside her shoulder so she could wrap it around her ribs. Held tight, but free to look somewhere other than his watchful gaze. He saw way too much for her comfort. She didn't need him watching her figure out a way to get past his defenses.

What was he so worried she'd ask for, anyway? His love? She wasn't that foolish. A permanent place in his life? She wasn't that brave. But…

"Will you tell me what happened? What finally sent you home?"

He didn't move. Didn't even seem to breathe.

"You can tell me to leave you alone, but…" She bit her lip, dredging up the courage. "I won't ask you to love me, but it'd be enough if you could trust me." If he could trust *anyone*. "You need someone to hear your secrets. Someone you know will keep them."

"Why?" A serious question. It meant he was listening, finally.

"Because secrets are poison." She knew, more than she could ever say to him. "They kill you a drop at a time, burning a hole inside until there's nothing left. I don't want that to happen to you. My biggest fear, the one that scares me more than anything, is that one day I'll look at you and you won't be there. I've lost everything else. Don't ask me to give you up, too."

The silence at her back stretched so long, she was sure he was about to shove her away. She braced herself for it. Waiting…

"There was a boy. Khushal. We found him working in a poppy field. There were a lot of kids there. Scared. Hungry. If I could have pulled them all, I would have, but we weren't allowed to interfere that way. The point of our missions was to recon supply routes. Find and disable any and all IEDs along the way. Bombs," he clarified, his arm tightening around her.

"Khushal was eight, maybe nine. Smart, too. He'd trade us info for food. Keep an eye out with us for his keepers. I didn't trust him at first, no one did. You can't trust anyone, really. But we passed his area a few times and he was always reliable."

He'd liked the boy. She knew this story wouldn't end well, so that knowledge felt like a stone in her throat. She pressed a kiss to his biceps, twining her fingers with his at her ribs.

"The others warned me. They said from the beginning,

it's the nice ones you have to worry about. The ones who hate you openly, those ones you know how far you can throw them. It's the ones who smile that are usually most interested in cutting your throat. I didn't listen. I thought I could tell for myself. I was wrong."

If she cried, he'd think she was pitying him, but it was so hard to keep it in. They'd taken a boy who'd wanted only to protect the innocent and made it impossible for him to believe in anything or anyone again. The worst part was, it was actually for his own good.

"We were on our way home when it happened. I was at the rear with Cade, talking about enemy positions in the mountains. Cushman was the first one to see him and we knew something was wrong. We stopped. He kept coming closer. Khushal *never* left his fields. Not on his own.

"He was there because he'd helped us. Because they knew we'd try to help him. Or at least that we wouldn't shoot him on sight. That *I* wouldn't. Because of that, none of the others did, either. We just stared at him. Beaten. Bloodied. Terrified. I can't forget his face. I never forget his face. He was so relieved he'd found us. He thought we'd save him. But all we could do was watch."

The tears slipped out against her will. Each word he uttered was filled with more and more anger. Not at the child. That poor boy had been a victim. A victim that haunted him.

"He exploded before we could even try. Before any of us realized what he was. They put enough shit on that kid to turn a fucking tank inside out. One second Khushal was there, the next…nothing but fire. No air. No sky. Nothing. Just fire.

"I got up, grabbed Cade and dragged him to some rocks.

Put out the fire on his pack. I went back for the others, there just wasn't much to go back to. Cush was dead. The part of him I did find, his face and chest were…gone. Roarke and Galindo were burning. Completely engulfed. Still screaming, somehow. Chavez was still alive. His legs were gone. Most of his hips. What was left was sizzling."

She turned her face into his arm. She would have wrapped both arms around him but he was holding her too tight. His body was rigid behind her, but now that he'd started, she could tell he couldn't stop. He was back there, looking at those poor men. Feeling it all over again.

"He begged me… Begged me to end it. He was my brother. I couldn't leave him like that. Couldn't leave any of them that way."

God. She knew. What he'd done. What he'd had to do. A choice that wasn't a choice.

"I didn't know until it was over that shrapnel from the blast had hit me. That I was still burning."

The surgical lines on his belly. The scarred skin on the back of his arm. Across the upper part of his back…

"Cade brought me back. He all but dragged me those last five miles. We were under fire after the explosion. He's the only reason we made it back at all. Said he wasn't watching another brother die and I knew I couldn't do it, either. I owed it to him to get him back. I covered him, he covered me. All that mattered was getting him home. I didn't care what happened to me once we made it to base. But I should never have come out of that hospital."

"Rick—"

"Everything decent about me, everything that ever made sense… I died there, Whit. I killed my brothers and I died there, in the middle of that *fucking* dirt road. So, no matter how good you are to me, no matter how much you make me wish it was different… There's nothing left of me to give you."

She couldn't hold the sob in. She struggled, forcing him to let her turn to him, wrapping both her arms around his neck, the tears ripping from her now. She held him as tight as she could, crying because she knew he *couldn't*.

"You're not dead," she whispered, kissing his jaw, his lips. "You don't *deserve* to be dead, either. It was mercy, Rick. You gave them mercy."

He shook his head, pulling her hands off.

"Yes. You're not dead. I'll tell you every day, every chance I get, until you hear me. You're. Not. Dead."

He looked at her, not quite enraged, but fighting her. He had her hands between them now, refusing the embrace.

Still, she held on. "You're not on that road anymore. You're here. With me. No matter what we've been through, remember? *You* said that. Always."

"God—" He tried to pull himself away, but she kept him the only way she knew how. She kissed him again. Not sensually. Not meaning to seduce. It was simply her entire heart, there for him to feel.

He stopped fighting, going completely still in that way he had, as if she'd think he'd disappeared. Or that she'd give up. She only held on tighter. Seconds passed before she finally felt him begin to relax. Increment by increment, the tension in him ebbed away.

He pulled back with a soft, resigned sigh. "There really is nothing that will make you give up on me, is there?"

He was finally learning. "Not even my last breath."

He stared at her. Not angry. Not demanding. Not even

with lust, which really, she would have been okay with. He just looked at her as if he truly didn't have the first clue what to say.

Finally, after thirty years, she won an argument.

The moment didn't last long. Something on his bedstand beeped. They both looked. Phone, keys, badge, and gun. It all rested on a tray in front of the lamp. She didn't think it was her imagination when she saw a flash of relief cross his face.

"I have to take that." He twisted to find the phone. A slide of his thumb on the phone's screen and he answered with a curt "Trelane." He listened a second, his gaze cutting to her before he sat up fully. "You're sure?"

A few more exchanges and he climbed out of the bed, deliciously nude and completely uncaring about it as he stalked to his closet. Her gaze found the burn scars, patches across his back and arms. More scars, like the bullet wounds on his chest and shoulders. Another knife wound in the upper part of his back. Curiously, another tattoo she'd never seen right next to it.

It was of a knife, pointed downward, its handle connected to what looked like a set of brass knuckles. An elaborate hilt, reminding her of eagle's wings spread out. Above the entire design, in bold capital letters, read USMC. All around the blade: "Hard To Kill." The graceful touch, she thought, was the ribbon across the blade's center. It was too small to read, but she could see the shape. There was only one thing that looked like that: Semper Fi.

He disappeared inside the closet, though she could still hear him giving orders and pulling things off hangers. She sat up, tucking the sheet and blankets under her arms and wiping her cheeks with her hands. Saved by the co-worker.

She couldn't really blame him for taking the distraction. He must feel like a raw wire and she wasn't going to push more than she already had, anyway. The gift of his trust meant more than she could ever say. She wouldn't betray it by demanding more.

He came back, replacing his phone on the bed stand, and began rooting around in a drawer for something as he tossed a fresh uniform on the bed. "We should shower and get out of here."

We? Not that she asked it, since her tongue was tied at the sight of him heading toward the ensuite bathroom. At least she managed to say, "Out?"

"I have to go back to the station and I don't think you want to go home looking like you just got out of my bed."

"Oh, sure, like anyone will believe *that*."

That seemed to stop him in his tracks. Before she could ask what was wrong, he stalked to the bed and scooped her right up against him so they were nose to nose. "You're going to stop putting yourself down. Especially in front of me."

"But I wasn—"

"It stops, Whitney. Right now." He glared at her, unblinking, and this time, she knew no argument in the world would be allowed. She nodded, receiving a fast kiss in reward. "Good. Now, you coming on your own or do I have to carry you?"

"I can walk, He-Man." Though, as soon as the words were out, she realized walking around naked—in bright light—was quite a bit different than lying under blankets that way. When he seemed to take exception to her hesitation, she yelped, "Why do you have to go in again?"

He got up, now one hundred percent put upon male,

taking her hand and tugging her out of the bed. "A suspect in Brody's murder was arrested down in Norco. They're going to let us question him."

She stumbled a little at the change of topic. "You have a suspect?"

"A few." Literally dragged into the bathroom, she soon found herself herded into a shower stall. "I'll let you know what we find. For now, we have about fifteen minutes to get going."

The water turned on with a quick slash of his hand, the blast hitting him in the back as he crowded her to the wall. The look in his eyes was definitely not focused on his work. Instead, he was staring at her breasts again, his big hand settling on her waist. *Uh oh.* "Fifteen minutes isn't very long."

"I'm a Marine, Whit." He lifted her, the warm water sluicing over his shoulder and hitting her thigh as she instinctively wrapped her legs around his waist. She gasped, holding on to him when he leaned in to kiss her. "I'm all about time management."

Chapter Eleven

Rick walked into the station, heading straight to his office to grab his files and a fresh legal pad. Schraeder would be driving down with him and since Whitney had absolutely no respect for a clock, he was already running late. He still wasn't ready to think too much on what had happened between them, but he did have the disconcerting sense that the world wasn't as heavy as it had felt just the day before. He knew he'd be thinking about that fact all night long.

Normally, they'd have waited until morning to go down and talk to Lucas Wainwright, but Schraeder's connection was on now and his captain was willing to let them take a crack at the bastard. They would only have him twenty-four hours for questioning. Less, if he lawyered up about the bookmaking charge. Sure he had the necessities, Rick nearly stepped out, but he stopped when he heard the deps talking.

"It's just ten minutes, Henderson." Schraeder, already irritated.

"Ten minutes to us, yeah. Not him. That's hours to him. You know that man is only late if someone breaks both his legs and maybe hits him with a car."

It had been a truck, actually. And only one broken leg. The other breaks had been ribs, fingers, and an arm. Not that Henderson or any of the others had been around when that happened, which is why they all laughed. It was just a story to them.

"Maybe you *interrupted* him?" Henderson's suggestive tone didn't need much interpretation.

"Yeah," Schraeder replied sarcastically. "That *had* to be it. Couldn't have been that he was sleeping or anything. You're such an asshole, man."

"What? Chicks dig him. You'd do him, wouldn't you, De?"

"Hell, yeah. In a heartbeat," de la Santos gave an off-hand reply. Rick knew Marines and the women never turned down a chance to slam an idiot in the balls. Especially when that idiot all but laid them on the table and handed over a hammer. "He'd *never* get all sobby and beg afterward like you do."

More laughter.

"Hey, who looks worse there? The crier or the one who bangs criers?"

"The crier," everyone replied remorselessly.

"Fuck all you," Henderson laughed.

"Well, we can't say you haven't tried," Schraeder threw out.

"Seriously, though," Henderson unwisely began again. "You *know* you didn't wake him up. Guys that wound up don't sleep. And did you see him walk in? I know *that* walk and I'm telling you, someone got laid."

Okay. That was it. Rick stepped out silently, turning the corner to stand in clear view. It took no time for most of them to spot him, especially de la Santos standing by the coffee machine. Suddenly, everyone had something fascinating to look at on their desks. Henderson, unfortunately for him, was sitting on his desk, his back to the corner where Rick stood.

"Looks more like someone's getting shot." De la Santos lifted her mug in mock salute before walking off to her desk. "Been nice knowing you, Hen."

Henderson was at least smart enough not to run, hanging his head but not otherwise moving from his perch. "I'm pulling shit shifts until I'm dead, aren't I?"

And any other crap work Rick could think up would be piled on him too. "Probably long after, too," Rick replied low enough that no one else would hear. The kid was excellent in his duties, but he had no idea how to keep his mouth shut. This might be a good lesson for him.

He nodded to Schraeder, who grabbed his coat off the back of his chair and followed Rick to the truck outside. Best part? Schraeder didn't ask a single question on the ride to Norco.

They were greeted by Schraeder's friend, Thompson, and his captain, who Rick could see sizing them up before they even got out of the truck. He introduced himself as Captain Aaron Stensen, gave a firm handshake, and had a brusque demeanor that fit his older-man, seen-too-much-of-this-crap expression. Easily in his fifties, Rick had no doubt he probably had.

He spoke while leading them to the interrogation rooms. "You can have an hour. If you can get him on anything, you can have him. I don't expect you to, though. He's not talking."

"Lawyer?" Schraeder asked, though none of them were surprised.

"No, Wainwright hates lawyers. He only keeps his busy in court. He's just not saying anything."

"Drove all the way out here, might as well take a shot," Rick said, nodding in thanks. Worst case scenario, word of Wainwright's interview would get out—he'd make sure of that—and attention in town about Brody's murder would shift away from Whitney. Best case scenario, the bastard would confess out of the goodness of his heart.

They entered the interrogation room, which contained only a few things: a table, four chairs, a camera on the wall, and a big, shaggy looking man smoking a cigarette. Unfiltered, Rick noted with longing. He'd had to quit when he was in the hospital and it hadn't been worth it to start up again, not with Whitney constantly slapping them out of his hand. The relentless woman had made it her personal mission to keep him healthy, whether he liked it or not.

Damn it, now was not the time to get distracted.

He refocused on Wainwright, who brought that damn cigarette to his mouth, watching them insolently while he pulled in a deep drag. Mid- to late-twenties, maybe a shade over six feet. Strong enough, but no beast. Carelessly grown black hair fell in the suspect's face, parting in the middle and jaggedly reaching past the shoulder line. His face wasn't very remarkable, thin and long and pale, but his dark eyes had a sharp, assessing stare Rick reminded himself to stay aware of. His beat up black duster and simple black shirt didn't scream successful loan shark, but it was hard to say what would. Other than that stare. This guy had a long game planned. Possibly a *very* long game.

Okay then.

Rick dropped his manila folder on the table and took his seat in front of the suspect. Schraeder positioned himself against the wall, right next to the door. Arms crossed, face appropriately blank.

Wainwright, however, just looked bored. His booted foot was on the chair next to him, his smoking arm rested on his raised knee. "You guys are here about Brody, right?"

So much for not talking. Rick nodded once, not taking his eye off the suspect.

"'Bout fuckin' time." Wainwright flicked his ash in an empty styrofoam cup on the table. "I've been waiting in here forever."

"You want us to believe you knew we were coming from Marketta tonight?"

"Guy dies thirty minutes after I talk to him and they come up with some bullshit so they can drag me in for a chat? I can do the math, Sheriff. Figured it's better to get it out of the way, since I don't need you up my ass from now to eternity. If you want to ask anything worth answering, now's the time."

"Did you kill Brody Roberts?" Might as well start with the big one.

Wainwright grinned, took another drag. "No."

Well, he knew it wouldn't be that easy. "But you admit you were with him that night?"

"Yeah."

Great, this was going to be one of *those* sessions. This dick was going to make him drag out every little word. "You want to elaborate on that?"

If he said no, he was getting shot.

Thankfully, Wainwright seemed to put that together. "We occasionally do business together."

"Any debts involved in that business?"

"A few. Nothing major. Brody came to me about a year and a half ago, needed some startup capital."

"I've seen Brody's financials. Why would you give him money when the banks wouldn't?"

"Banks don't enforce payment by handing a man a jar full of his own teeth."

"But you do?"

A non-answering smile.

Moving on. "How did you meet Brody?"

"I had a previous investment with a friend of his. The guy took artsy pictures of naked women. It made good money, so it was worth it for me when they came up with another idea."

Rick opened his folder and pulled out the enlarged print out of Jason Dewar's license picture. He turned it around and slid it over to Wainwright. "This him?"

"Yeah, that's Jason."

"You seen him lately?"

"Jason?" Wainwright seemed genuinely surprised at that one. "No. I usually don't see either of them. They pay my dividends every month to my account and as long as they do, neither of them needs to see me. Ever."

"Dividends." Rick leaned back in his seat. He stared at Wainwright for a long moment, weighing his next set of questions. "You're some kind of silent partner in their business?"

"You could say that. I was the original bankroll. Hundred and fifty grand for equipment, set up, and advertising. I keep a one-third stake. I knew that shit would pay for itself and it did."

"So, you knew what kind of business this was." Rick felt more than heard when Schraeder shifted against the wall. He turned his head, just enough, in Schraeder's direction to stop him.

Wainwright glanced over, suspicion flickering on his face, but he answered Rick anyway. "Sure I did. Some kind of titty peep show site. People paying for porn. It's not new and like I said, it pays for itself. They were able to get content from other production places and produce some themselves. They handle the business, I get paid. It's a no-brainer investment."

Clearly. "Did you ever check in on that investment?"

"I checked in on my money," Wainwright answered glibly. "My assistant verified that the site was live from time to time, other than that, no. I don't spend a lot of time screwing around on the computer for tits and ass, man. I get that for real whenever I want."

"We're going to need to contact your assistant, make sure he can corroborate your story."

"Danny?" Wainwright huffed, amused. "Sure, you can talk to Danny. Doubt he'll remember anything though. He's an idiot."

Rick stopped making his note on the legal pad. "You allow idiots to check on your money?"

"Hell no." Wainwright stretched his leg out. "My sister's kid. All he does is make coffee and get in my way all day. I let him take care of the easy things. Pushing papers, taking out trash. He's handy for weeding out people bugging me for dumb shit, though. Get on a phone with Danny for ten minutes, trust me... You don't call back if you don't have to." Wainwright seemed to enjoy the prospect of sharing his irritating relation with the police.

"The meeting in Marketta the night Brody died?"

"His idea." Stubbing out his dead smoke, Wainwright reached for his half-empty pack with his other hand. He lit a new one from the book of matches on the table, shaking out the flame with a flick of his wrist. "He wanted to talk to me about setting up some security."

Interesting. "Digital security?"

Wainwright's cheeks sucked in deep, followed by a thick cloud of smoke between them. Damn it, the smell made his mouth itch. "Physical. He was worried about some crazy bastard stalking him."

Disbelief twitched at the back of Rick's neck. "*Brody Roberts* asked for physical security?"

Wainwright's harsh chuckle agreed, which didn't help the twitch at all. "That's what I said. That sonbitch was a brick shithouse, but he wanted *me* to find people to watch out for his ass? I couldn't believe he dragged me all the way up there for that, but he was so damn paranoid, he didn't want to risk getting caught out on the road."

This was news. Brody had always been overconfident, a physical bully. For him to admit fear… "Did he say anything specific about the stalker?"

"That's all he talked about. Some crazy old guy who wanted his daughter's videos off the site."

Mark Gorski.

"The guy was obsessed, something about the daughter being dead and he wasn't giving up 'til they were the same way. Brody said he was getting phone calls, thought someone was breaking into his place. He swore he was being followed."

"You didn't believe him?" Rick made more notes. Maybe Brody *had* been stalked. If Gorski was the killer, that would fit right in with his threats. Where the hell was Hughes' contact in San Francisco?

"Are you kidding? When they built that site, the deal was that *no one* would be traceable directly. The last thing I need is some skank's dad chasing me because she blew someone on camera."

They had themselves a real sweetheart here. "They actually promised you that? That no one would be able to trace you?" Smart as Lucas Wainwright seemed to think he was, Rick was surprised at how little the man knew about the business he'd involved himself with.

Rick's prey seemed to pick up on his disdain. Wainright's face had a distinct "fuck you" stamp to it now. "Damn right they did. I wasn't about to give them anything if they didn't. You think I *want* to get hassled about stupid shit? Dumb fuck's one job was to handle anything like this himself and leave me out of it."

So, that was what Brody brought to the deal. He was supposed to be the muscle. "Brody was never behind the camera?"

Wainwright snorted out smoke. "*Hell* no. Jason was the cameraman. No one trusted Brody with actual equipment. Maybe a GoPro, but that's it." He laughed at his own joke. When they didn't join him, he explained with his lips clamping the cigarette so he could outline a small square with his hands. "You know, those cameras in a box. People strap 'em to their heads and do stupid shit, like jump off cliffs and bridges?" Still getting no reaction, he shrugged his shoulders and went back to smoking. "You two need to get out more."

"Yeah," Rick replied, not really caring. "We'll get right on that."

The assessing stare was back. "You're kind of an asshole, aren't you?" Wainwright asked, decidedly too comfortable for Rick's tastes.

"There's no *kind of* about it." Something this idiot would find out once the interrogation was over. "Witnesses at the bar say you were fighting with him."

Wainwright's disgust was unmistakable. "You ever spend more than twenty minutes with that shithead?"

Rick allowed another nod.

Wainwright, cigarette still between two fingers, gestured a point with them. "Then you *know*."

"More than you realize," he agreed solemnly. "What did you fight about?"

"It wasn't a fight. Mostly some yelling. He pissed me off, so I told him to cover his own ass. He called me some names and then he left. Last I saw him, he was following some chick to the bathroom. I finished my beer and I left. Simple as that."

"Simple as that," Rick repeated. No way was it simple as that. "Word on the street is you had a marker on him for two hundred grand."

Another snorted laugh. "Brody Roberts wasn't worth shit. Why would I give anyone that kind of money for *him*?"

A good question, but one Rick thought he might have an answer for. "He'd be worth it if he was screwing you over."

Wainwright's eyes narrowed and his lips flattened. Not a lot, but more than enough to be a tell.

"What's the matter, Lucas? You find out how much the site was *really* making?" Rick put the picture of Dewar back in the folder, laying his hand flat on top. "Brody probably knew you weren't keeping too good an eye on the site itself. He was lazy, yeah, but he was also smart. Especially when it came to money and keeping more than his share of it. What'd he want, to buy you out completely? Get rid of you once he didn't need you anymore?"

The truth of that statement was as clear as the frown on Wainwright's face.

"You're not about to leave your nice, comfortable territory to make Brody feel better about a stalker, but I *do* think you'd drag your ass up to Marketta to get your hands on him if he was fucking with your income. I think that kind of stupidity is right up your alley."

"I didn't kill him." The smooth operator's mask had slipped away, leaving only the angry thug starting to realize the corner he was in.

"It's not looking that way, Lucas." If it had just been Brody, that might be true. Unfortunately, Wainwright didn't seem to know Dewar was dead, too. And there was no indication he had a woman working close enough to him for murder. Yet.

"I have proof."

Rick stared at him, waiting. Wainwright didn't seem willing to part with it, grimacing while he stubbed out his second cigarette. "I don't got all night, Lucas." Just twelve more minutes.

The bastard still took his damn time. "My phone. I recorded my conversation with him." Because he was still smart enough not to trust Brody.

"The phone you surrendered when you were arrested?"

Wainwright clammed up. "I want my lawyer."

Rick nodded easily enough. "You're gonna need him."

He looked to Schraeder, who opened the door. Thompson came in, a smile on his face that immediately made Wainwright nervous. "You can arrest him now."

Thompson advanced and Wainwright stood up, toppling his chair. "Fuck you, he's not arresting me."

"I'd do it," Rick replied calmly while Thompson grabbed their struggling suspect's arms to put the cuffs on. "But we're outside my jurisdiction." And Rick wasn't sure he wouldn't accidentally beat the shit out of Wainwright on principle.

"I didn't do nothing!" he yelled, struggling even though the metal was tight around his wrists.

"Lucas Wainwright, you're under arrest for the production, possession, sale, and distribution of child pornography," Thompson began, sending Wainwright into an outright panic. "You have the right to remain silent…"

Rick stopped listening, steering clear of the other officers who'd come in to help control Wainwright and take him down to booking. He picked up his folder and legal pad, and tucked his pen back in his chest pocket. Schraeder leaned back on the table, a small smile on his face. "You kept him so focused on avoiding a murder charge, he walked right into the website."

Rick shook his head. "That's not entirely true. He had no idea what the website was doing." Or not doing. They'd used the court order to tear it down direct from the hosting site days ago.

Schraeder crossed his arms again. "Doesn't make him any less guilty to me."

Not to Rick, either. Wainwright didn't care what Brody and Dewar were doing. It was no better than loading a weapon and leaving it where children would find it.

"It's still good work, Chief."

Rick looked up and nodded. One less asshole preying on desperate people, anyway. The legalities about the site would fall into the hands of the lawyers now. His men would keep investigating details and digging up more facts to put the nails in Wainwright's coffin. Now, his job was to solve the murders of Wainwright's partners.

"I'm betting they'll get more from that phone than just Wainwright bitching about Brody." Odds were good Wainwright had provided enough nails all by himself. Rick was curious, though, if there was some truth to the stalker story. The best lies were couched firmly in the truth.

"You believe him about not being the killer?"

Much as he didn't want to admit it, he did. "He never would have left us a body to find. And he thinks Dewar is still alive."

"So, what's our next move?"

Wasn't that the big question? But for Schraeder's purposes, he knew what to say. "Go home. Find Gorski. Put this thing to bed."

"Gorski might be another of Wainwright's lies."

"First rule you have to learn about this job–everyone lies. Usually, for the dumbest damn reasons you'll ever hear. Your job is digging the truth out from the middle of them. So, we start with the lie and work from there."

Schraeder blinked a few times, his face thoughtful. "Gorski it is, then."

Yeah, this one was going to work out just fine.

Chapter Twelve

The dream had her in its claws again. The blackness, being unable to breathe with her face shoved into the bedding. Hands, cruel and bruising, touching her everywhere. Pulling. Yanking. Shoving. Pain. God, the pain. Stabbing into her, tearing, ripping her apart. She screamed, but there was no sound. There never was. Only their grunts, their yells, their laughter. Growing louder and louder, drowning out her—

Her scream echoed through the living room as she sat up on the couch, tangled in her blankets, sweat pasting her hair to her forehead, her sleeveless nightgown to her body. Gasping, choking for breath that her lungs couldn't seem to take in. But somehow, she was sobbing, shaking so hard she thought she would fall.

"It's okay, Aunt Whitney. It's okay. You're safe now." Strong hands held hers, one of them brushing her hair back. Wiping the tears away. Alison. She focused on her niece's face, her erratic heartbeat thundering in her ears. Calm.

Alison was always so calm when the dreams were this bad. She continued to speak, soft and low, letting Whitney pull her close and hold on. The hands that smoothed up and down her back were almost maternal. "You're with me now. You're safe."

Safe? No, not here she wasn't. Not like she'd felt with—"Oh, God, Rick…" He wasn't here, was he?

The hands on her back stilled. "*Me*, Aunt Whitney. Alison. *I'm* here, not him. Just like always."

Whitney nodded, holding tight onto Alison's hand, relieved when she felt the soothing strokes down her back again. Little by little, she felt herself come back into the present, hating herself for this weakness she couldn't seem to get rid of. The fear. The fucking terror of it. She'd thought, stupidly now, that what had happened the night before with Rick meant she'd gotten past it. But the dream was back, more viciously than before. Why? Why couldn't she just make it go away?

"They're gone now," Alison said. "They can't hurt you anymore."

The morning after it had happened, Alison had found her sobbing in her bed. She had done then what she was doing now. Firmly telling Whitney what she needed to get grounded again. And as she had that horrible morning, Whitney wondered what horrors the girl had been through, that she knew what to do to pull herself together. Alison was the one who'd helped her to the shower, to wash off the blood and the sweat, the stink of them. She'd gone with her to the clinic, to make sure the damage was treated. And when the dreams came, Alison was there to bring her back from the edge.

A child should never have to be the one to shelter the adult. She'd never wanted to do this to anyone, not after having been through it herself with her own mother. She hated doing it to Alison. So much. She pulled herself out of the girl's grasp, shaking her head at Alison's questioning glance.

"Don't be ashamed," Alison said softly, watching Whitney with those dark eyes that seemed to have seen too much. "You did what you had to do."

Whitney winced.

"They're dead, you don't have to worry about them coming back ever again."

She knew Alison was trying to be reassuring, but her words made it worse. "It doesn't matter. They're still in my head. I'm still afraid." She was still hiding. Lying, to herself, to Rick. Pretending she could walk away from the past and the truth and the ugliness of her choices.

Choices that weren't choices.

Responsibilities she resented.

Guilt she couldn't ignore.

She'd made the choice to hide and just like she'd told Rick, the secret was eating at her. Rapaciously devouring her soul. Stealing anything good in her life and twisting it.

No more.

No more hiding. No more running. No more living with a monument to her fear in her own damn house. She wiped her tears with her hands.

"Alison?" Strange, how normal her own voice sounded, when inside, she was nearly vibrating. Anger, rage, violence, it felt like an eruption growing inside her. An explosion just waiting to go off.

Her niece straightened, watching her carefully.

"Go to the pantry and get one of the boxes there. Then, go to my room and get all the pictures out of it. Every single one." She didn't wait for the girl to move. She yanked at the tangle of bedding, kicking herself free. Alison barely seemed to get out of her way before she stalked to the kitchen and out through the back door. Cold morning air slapped her in the face, arms, and feet, but Whitney hardly felt the sting. What she needed was at the back of the yard, just before the grass gave way to the line of trees that had stood longer than she'd been alive. She stalked barefoot through the grass, all the way to the stump where the firewood had been chopped into pieces. Her hand found the long handle of the axe, wrapped around it with familiarity. She grasped it with both now, pulling it free with a hard wrest. The blade was sharp, almost as sharp as her intentions.

She looked back at the house. At the windows of her bedroom. At the nightmare that had happened in there. Then, she headed back into the house.

No more.

• • •

"Mark Gorski hasn't been seen by anyone he knows for at least the last three weeks."

It was not the news Rick wanted to hear first thing that morning. He'd been driving when Hughes called his cell, pulling into his destination with a heavy sigh. He took the captain off speaker. Hughes continued talking, outlining how his contact in San Francisco had been trying to find some kind of trace of the man, but all they had were some pretty shitty facts that only made the whole thing worse.

"Gorski's life fell apart when his youngest daughter died about six months ago. Car accident. That's also about the time the website started getting emails from him. He finally lost his job about two months ago, reportedly due to repeated problems with alcohol. Several disorderly conduct arrests are on record during that period, too. He was a janitor at a middle school up there and they couldn't have that around the kids. And he was in the midst of a civil lawsuit against the driver of the car that killed his daughter."

"Civil?" Rick picked his hat up off the seat next to him. "There were no criminal charges brought?"

"The daughter was hit by the son of a prominent judge. Odds weren't good that there was going to be much justice for the daughter in civil court, either, but the old man was determined to try. His neighbors said before the accident, he'd been one of the most decent people they knew. Wife died years before. Oldest daughter is estranged, apparently. There wasn't anyone to keep him together afterward."

"Shit." There wasn't much else to say about it. Gorski had taken hit after hit. It was no wonder he'd snapped. "What do we know about the daughters?"

"Not much about the older one. She lives somewhere in New Jersey according to Gorski's neighbors, hasn't been home in over ten years. Turns out the younger one was a wannabe actress for a short time. She'd been living down here in So Cal for about three years, trying to make a go of it. Did some modeling, got a few commercials, even. Then last year, she went back home and never looked back."

Rick didn't want to think about it but the ugly facts couldn't be ignored. "Dewar. She met Dewar."

"SF sent me her picture, I cross-referenced her to find

the videos her father wanted taken down. She's in the stills Dewar took in his studio shots." Hughes voice went so low it was a whisper. "I found her in the rape section, too."

The silence on the line stretched out long, but Rick couldn't think of any way to fill it.

"I've never seen anything like this, Chief. I don't know what to do with it."

He wished he had some answers for the kid that would help. "We do what we can. We do the *best* we can and we try to live with the rest." Try. That was the important word there. "I wish I had some magic words to make it easier for you, but I don't."

"I know, sir." But he didn't. Rick could tell he didn't. Hughes was steadfast and damn good at what he did. He just hadn't gotten very adept at putting the shit of it all to the side. He'd never last if he couldn't get out from under the weight of it.

"You know why I do this, Hughes? Why I didn't put down my guns and do anything I could find that wasn't enforcement?" There were any number of things he could have done. His cousin had a construction company he could have worked for. He had technical skills, he could have gone into teaching. But none of that was an option for him. "Because there's a hell of a lot of death and murder and violence in the world. Some of it, I put there. There's not a lot of justice, though. I can't stop the other things. No matter how hard I try, I can't and that was a hard realization to come to—but I *can* find justice for some of it. I may not sleep much, but when I do, that's how I do it."

He could hear Hughes trying to come up with a way to answer him. Some things didn't need an answer. Or just didn't have one.

He signed off and grabbed his hat. Then he climbed out, slamming the door and staring at the small building that was almost as much a home as the house he'd grown up in. His father's clinic.

This had to be done, but it wasn't easy to face doing it. Only Richard Trelane could make him feel like he was eight years old again, hiding a secret that would get him in trouble. His father never frightened him. But, Rick acknowledged as he took that first step from the road to the curb, the idea of disappointing the man felt like a blade between his ribs.

Determined to get it over with, nervousness thrumming through him, he walked into the clinic, glad to see there weren't any patients in the waiting room. Anna, his father's long suffering nurse, sat at the front desk, glaring down at her crossword puzzle.

She glanced up distractedly as he took off his hat, dropping her glasses to their safety chain with a double take when she recognized him. "Little Ricky Trelane, as I live and breathe!"

He had to smile as she came around the counter to hug him. "No one has called me that since second grade."

"No one else out there changed your diapers, so I can call you what I want." She gave him a matronly squeeze, patting his chest when she pulled back, blinking madly and sniffing away her almost-tears. It was close, but the tough older woman reined her emotions in like a seasoned soldier. "I was starting to think you'd never come visit."

Probably because he never thought he would, either. "I need to see him."

"You picked a good day. We've got a clear schedule."

She pointed him toward the office at that end of the hall. Not much had changed inside, the patient rooms still lined up on the left, the open bathroom and scale on the right. It looked like the longest fifteen feet of his life.

"Anna, did I hear—" The door to the office swung open and suddenly his father was there, eyes widening in surprise. "Rick."

"Dad." They stared at each other for a tense minute. They'd seen each other over the years, of course, but it was always strained. A visit to the house on those rare occasions he needed something stored there. Occasionally passing each other in town. There were fewer than four thousand people in Marketta, it was impossible not to see each other.

Richard pulled himself together first. "C-come in, I'm just back here looking at files."

The office had seemed a lot larger when he was a kid, Rick realized, ducking a bit as he came through the door. Or maybe it was the stacks of boxes and piles of folders filling just about every available space that made the place feel cramped. Richard was already behind the desk by the time Rick entered, so he closed the door quietly before dropping into the only empty guest chair. He looked around, trying to cap his tension and nerves, holding his hat on his knee with a frown. "This place is worse than *my* office."

His father laughed uneasily. "Your mother always said I was secretly a hamster."

An unexpected half laugh broke free when Rick thought of his mother and her complaints about his father's books in the den. "You're saying we're both hoarders?"

"How about *paper-inclined*? In my defense, we're preparing all these records to be digitized. Anna's determined to drag me into the twenty-first century. Something about reducing her danger of dying in a fire." His father's warm gaze settled on his face and Rick felt the longing in it. Usually, it made him painfully uncomfortable but he pushed down the insecurity. "So, what brings you by?"

Rick cleared his throat, trying to think of an answer that wouldn't open a whole other can of worms. He just didn't have one. He shook his head, raising his hand in a helpless shrug. "Whitney."

His dad nodded, saying her name at the same time. "She's beautifully determined, that one. Always telling me I should consider waking up a little earlier in the morning for breakfast. I've never had the heart to tell her she's too sweet to be truly pushy."

In what world? "You're just blinded by all those cinnamon rolls you like to order."

"They are amazing cinnamon rolls." A sheepish smile put some color in the older man's cheeks. "You didn't, ah, tell her about the picture, did you?"

"She didn't tear you a new one this morning?"

Richard shook his head. "She didn't come in. Last I checked, the shop still hasn't opened."

Rick looked down at his watch, frowning at the time. That was odd. She never missed a day of work. Of course, it was possible she'd slept in. Likely, even, given that dreamy smile she'd given him before driving away. That smile had stayed with him all night, following him into the few hours of sleep he did get, along with the scent of her from his pillows. Even now, he could still feel it pressed against his own lips—

"Ahh-haaaa!" Richard's pleased accusation made Rick look up. "You finally figured things out with Whitney. Thank

God, I was starting to worry you wouldn't ever get your act together."

He wasn't sure how to respond to that, though something that felt oddly like a smile tried to form on his face.

His father seemed to take that for acknowledgement, pounding lightly on his desk with glee. "I knew it! I knew you'd see what was right in front of you eventually."

"We haven't figured anything out yet, Dad." Not a single damn thing, actually.

"But there's a 'we.' That's a start."

Was it? Rick sighed, not wanting to break his father's bubble but… "There're a lot of problems to work through." None of which he could explain to his father without a breach of either professionalism or trust. But the laundry list of issues seemed to grow by the day.

And none of them were why he was here.

He looked at the man he'd expected to be like when he grew up, knew they were polar opposites in the ways that truly counted. His father had dedicated his life to preserving life. To taking away pain and doing everything in his power to keep the people healthy and safe. How much shame would he feel when he realized exactly how much death and pain his son had caused? How destructive he was to every life he'd ever touched. How would this man, whose respect Rick had always wanted to earn, ever look at him again if he knew?

Rick closed his eyes, swamped with a feeling he couldn't begin to describe as anything but wrong. He pinched the bridge of his nose with a sigh. "I have no fucking idea what I'm doing anymore."

He heard the squeak of his father's chair, the swish of

fabric as the man came to Rick's side of the desk and moved the stack of folders from the second chair. Rick looked over at him, not at all sure what the older man might do.

He didn't expect patient amusement on that familiar face. "That's probably the best thing I've ever heard you say."

Confused, Rick leaned away in his seat. "What?"

Richard nodded, stretching his legs out. "Even when you were little, you always knew exactly what you wanted to do, how to get it done. You'd set a goal, go out, and achieve it. Start all over again for the next thing. You get that from your mother. I used to make it a habit to mess up her plans as much as I could." He smiled, clearly nostalgic. "God, she hated that."

Rick had no idea where this was going, but he thought back, remembered his mother frustrated and yelling his father's name… It always somehow ended with her giggles or laughing kisses he pretended not to see.

"Life isn't supposed to be executed like a mission plan, son. Sure, it's good to have a direction. To aim for something that gives it meaning. But it's also supposed to have surprises and serendipity and something else that starts with an 's' that you weren't expecting."

"The only word that comes to my mind is shit." Lots and lots of pointless shit.

His dad just laughed. "Exactly!"

Rick blew out an irritated breath.

"Do you think when your mother met me, she immediately went and put it in her planner to get married and have a child? That she thought that's what would satisfy her life goals?"

Probably not, no. His parents had met in college. His father had been in pre-med and his mother was pursuing a history degree.

"She had a plan. She was going to get her Masters, use it to become a researcher in a museum, preserving historical documents and surrounding herself in a world full of philosophy and politics. She wanted to dedicate herself to the study of knowledge. That's the plan of hers I'm proudest of destroying. Can you imagine it? *Your* mother, trapped in a dusty museum all day, looking at papers and books and nothing else?"

His mother had become an elementary school teacher, surrounded by eager-to-learn kindergartners who smeared her with equal amounts of affection and finger-paint for nearly twenty years. She'd loved every moment of her career, all the children she'd been able to teach.

"She still met her goal, she just went about it in a completely unexpected way. A way she never would have imagined if I hadn't upended everything she thought she wanted to do."

Rick thought about Whitney and that cookie she'd snuck into his treat box. The way she always seemed to trick him into letting her do things for him, things that made him better. Calmer. "You think my not having a clue what I'm doing is good for me?"

Richard sobered a little, but his eyes still twinkled. "I think it means you're finally living your life, Rick. Not your plan, your *life*."

"And Whitney? What about *her* life?" He shook his head, wishing it were all as simple as his father seemed to believe. "She's in trouble, Dad. Trouble I'm not sure I can get her out of." Finding Gorski was imperative. But he'd be an idiot to think that would be enough. "Even if I can, that doesn't mean I won't still drag her down. That I won't—" He cut himself off, not able to say the words that would show his father exactly what he was.

Richard tilted his head in question.

"I'm no good for her." A shameful truth. "I'm no good for anyone." Including his father.

"Why not?"

Rick shook his head.

"Son, I'm no fool. I know some terrible things happened to you. Things that made you start to think you brought them on yourself. Losses and decisions that hang on your soul. I don't pretend to know what they are, but I know they happened. And I know how hard they are to carry."

He stared at his father, both hopeful and afraid of what the older man might see with that knowing gaze. For the first time, he saw the shadows in those twinkling eyes. Marks of regrets he never imagined the other man had.

"It's a heavy weight, being the one who does what has to be done. The one who has to decide when enough is enough. Weighing a life in the balance has a cost no one can know of until they go through it themselves. If I'd had the choice, I never would have wanted that for you. But it's who you are. It's why I've always been so proud of you."

"Dad—"

"It's also why I never pushed when you walked away."

Rick looked away, the shame in him so great it felt like a weight on his chest. "I didn't mean to hurt you." Even as the words came out, he heard Whitney. *Of course it's meant to hurt. That's how you shut people out.* Damn if the truth didn't sting. "I didn't want you to see what I'd become."

"I know." Just that. The simplest acceptance, but the force of it blasted open the walls inside him. His father leaned forward, his hand landing on Rick's shoulder and squeezing reassuringly. "I *see* you, Rick. I've always seen you and I've never had a moment's disgrace at the man you are. Right now, you're fighting to control the impossible. Trying to protect what's most important, even when it's breaking you up inside. I can't fight that battle for you, but I can tell you I'm on your side. No matter what you think you've become, you will always be my son."

Rick's eyes stung, moisture making his vision swim as he brought his own hand up to cover his father's. He wanted to say how much that meant to him, the implicit forgiveness more than he'd ever expected. All he could do was hold on tight, loosening his hold only when a thick chuckle pushed out. "I still don't know what to do about Whitney."

Richard patted him firmly before letting go and leaning back in his chair. "Love her. Same way you always have."

Rick jolted, turning to face the man, words failing him.

"Except better," Richard added with a grin. "Because you know about it now."

"But I don—" His throat strangled the words he almost said. Because they weren't true. There was no hiding from it anymore. He *did* love Whitney. It felt like a tuning rod had just resonated inside him. Right down the center of him, crumbling all the reservations he'd built to nothing. Pure and true, the truth refused to be buried. He loved her, so deep it felt like the core of his very existence.

But it didn't change anything.

She gave him a peace he still didn't deserve, willing to

take on his pain, his needs, even when they cost her dearly. She'd still give him everything of herself, and not expect anything in return. She would never *ask* for anything. And she'd be so easy to hurt, no matter how hard he'd try not to. How could that not terrify him? "I don't want to be the thing that finally breaks her."

His father nodded. "Then don't be. If you put her first, make her the priority in your life, make sure she knows how you feel…that's enough."

"Hell, Dad, most of the time I can't even tell myself how I feel." The lock in his soul felt blown apart, but it was still there. The only thing holding the worst at bay. "She needs more than that."

"Probably true. If anyone on earth needs protecting from herself, it's Whitney. She lays her heart right out there when people mean something to her and it's cost her every time. But don't you think maybe it's time someone did the same thing for her?"

Lay his heart out for her? He unfisted his hands, consciously forcing himself to relax. His heart wasn't full of sweetness like hers. His was dark, full of anger and guilt. Pain and self-recrimination. Could he really let all that out?

Or had he already? Not all of it, of course, but he'd shared his worst pain with her and still she'd held him. She'd held him *tight*.

The sound of reveille cut through the room, making his father jump. Shaking his head at the interruption, Rick answered his cell phone.

"There's good news and there's shitty news," Cade began unceremoniously. "The good news is, Whitney's gun cleared the preliminary tests for the murders."

"Both?" The relief was staggering. Or it would be if Cade hadn't prefaced it that way. "You're sure both victims were shot with the same gun?"

"According to Ballistics, it's likely. The marks on the casings are consistent. They still have more to do, but her weapon definitely wasn't it."

What he wouldn't give to end the call there. "The shitty news?"

Richard shifted in his seat, a scowl rippling his brow. Rick felt one doing the same to his own face.

Cade took too damn long to answer. "Her fingerprints are on the casings from the Dewar scene. I'm sorry, Rick. We're going to have to bring her in."

"No." Absolutely *fucking* no. "How the hell did you get a comparison?"

"She had to get printed when she applied to take over care of her niece. They stay on record. When they found clear prints, I had to allow it."

Rick gripped the wooden armrest of the chair he was in, the force of his hand nearly bending it. What he really wanted to do was smash the phone into it.

"I wish there was another way—"

"Give me a few hours," he ground out. "I'm heading out to Brody Roberts' place. I was going to see if I could find any evidence of the stalking Wainwright mentioned." They'd already picked the place clean, but he believed in being thorough. Especially when the angle of the investigation changed. "Just a few more hours, Cade. If I can't find anything, I'll bring her in myself."

The silence crackled, the strain of it making Rick grind his teeth.

"You have three hours. That's all I can do."

Rick blew out a breath, the reprieve small but it would have to be enough. It was more than anyone else would have given.

Richard watched him put his phone back in his pocket and stand. "I think now might be a good time to tell me what's really going on."

He shouldn't, especially with time so short. But he couldn't just walk away. They both cared about her. She was as much family to his father as she was to him. "Whitney's in trouble."

Understanding dawned. "Brody. They think she killed him?"

Rick nodded, putting his hat back on his head.

"You know she didn't."

Yes, he did. But they both knew she could have. That she probably should have.

"What are you going to do?"

The only thing that could save her. "Find proof someone else did."

His father followed him out to the truck. As Rick got in, Richard set his hands on the open window. "I'm cutting my day short. If you can't find what you're looking for…come by the house before you head to Whitney's."

He shook his head. "I may not be able to do that."

"I know, but I want to be there. For both of you."

Rick closed his eyes. He didn't think he could arrest Whitney.

His father squeezed his arm. "Go save her."

Fifteen minutes later, Rick found himself on the wasted land where Brody Roberts had lived. The only place he had a prayer of finding something to help Whitney.

He walked up to the trailer, checking out the possible points of entry. The windows were glass panes, turned by a gear on the inside to close or open a few inches for air. No one would fit through there. The front door had two dead bolts—one weathered and discolored, the other still shiny and new. The second lock lent some credence to the notion of Brody's paranoia, especially when both locks had small scratches around the key slot. A key might scratch the top or bottom of a keyhole, but not the sides of it. Not unless someone had been tampering with the locks. But had they gotten in? No way to know.

Pulling a blade from his pocket, he cut through the police tape keeping the door shut and pushed inside. He sighed. Same shithole, different day. The techs had cleared the rooms of being any kind of crime scene, but the search for evidence in the web site investigation had torn just about everything apart. Couch gutted, desk tossed, cabinets emptied. He looked around, trying to see past it.

If Gorski were trying to get in, what had he done that Brody noticed? It could have been anything, from moved objects to missing ones. If Gorski was really playing mind games, it could even have been taunts. He couldn't begin to guess. The important thing was, what did *Brody* do, other than add that lock, because of it?

They already knew Brody kept nothing about the site in his home. Nothing they'd been able to find, anyway. Lazy, he reminded himself, but not stupid. Brody would protect himself, but not in a way that would require too much effort on his part. There was definitely something hidden in this tin can. He just had to find it.

He scanned back and forth, but there was nowhere to hide anything in the metal walls. The cabinets, cheap plywood with dark paper veneer, likely weren't designed to have secret compartments. The skylight in the kitchen ceiling was cracked and opaque, but it definitely wasn't compromised. There was another, smaller skylight hatch above the couch. That one, he realized, noting the same spinning reel closure on one side, was a serious contender. Without knowing the dimensions of his suspect, though, he couldn't say for sure if Gorski could have used it to get into the trailer. But it'd be a perfect way to see inside undetected. And if the second daughter was working with the man… He remembered those heel prints in the dirt. Small feet. Someone dainty could easily have slipped in here from the roof. But would they find what they were looking for?

He looked down. Cheap linoleum lined the metal floor… that stood three feet off the ground. There was lots of space under there for Brody to store something. But, no. Brody wouldn't drag himself into the dirt to hide something, least of all on a regular basis. He checked the bathroom, coming to the same conclusion there. Nothing.

The last room, the bedroom, was a completely new ball game. The bed, built into a frame of drawers and cabinets, took up the far wall. Behind the mattress, there were sliding panels and built-in recessed lights. If he had an idea of what he was looking for, it would help. Since he didn't, he pulled open the first cabinet on the side of the bed and started testing the inside panels. Nothing moved, slid, or pulled away. One by one, he went through each cabinet, finding nothing. Less than nothing. Not shocking, but damn frustrating. Which is probably why, his hand inside the sliding cabinet, he used a little too much force on the bottom panel and pushed right through it. Pulling back with a snap, he immediately reached for the flashlight.

The light pierced the deep hole, likely all the way down to the trailer floor. He couldn't see what it was, but he could tell there was something at the bottom. Something unreachable from where he stood.

He pulled back, realizing the access had to be the panel behind the mattress. Shoving it off the box spring only took a booted second or two. He climbed back on the bed, searching the thin wood panel for the way Brody must have used to get in. It slid along its grooved track, just the tiniest bit. A jostle, pushing it deeper to one side, caused it to slip free on the opposite end. He pulled and the whole piece came free, revealing a trove behind the wall. A goddamn treasure trove. Handguns, three of them, along the length of a shelf. A laptop and three large shoe boxes, each one more full than the last. Discs in cases. Flash drives. Women's clothes...

He backed away, disgust dropping his stomach several inches. Three boxes of evil. Of violence. Of violation. God only knew what was on that computer... His mind flashed on Whitney, hands shaking as she stared at her bedroom door. He all but ran out to the door of the trailer, bile in his throat as he burst outside and down the few rickety wooden steps, dragging in deep gulps of air to push it back down.

It hadn't occurred to him before. It should have. It fucking *should have*. Brody was bastard enough, twisted enough, to have recorded her. To have made himself a trophy of what they did to her. The psychotic fuck...

The temptation to set the entire trailer on fire warred

with the need he felt to help the other victims he knew were in those boxes. Whitney wouldn't thank him for giving in to the inclination.

Do your job.

Her voice in his mind again. The conscience he didn't know he had.

Closing his eyes, he forced his breathing to slow down. Even out. It took a few minutes, but he eventually went back to the truck, pulling his evidence kit from the truck bed. Gritting his teeth, he made his way back to the overturned bed. He had to do this. Had to be the cold-blooded son of a bitch everyone accused him of being. He donned his latex gloves and pulled out his phone. Took pictures to document the find. One by one, he removed the boxes. The computer. He put the latter down on the box spring surface to be put in a large evidence bag. The clothes—underwear, mostly—he put in the first evidence bag directly. It was more important to preserve any physical evidence on them by not transfer-ring them to another surface.

The DVDs were in slim, clear cases and filled one entire box. Each one was labeled with a woman's name. Sometimes two. The last case in the box, however, stood empty, waiting for its next occupant. Nothing would ever fill that case, thank God. He shook his head, cleared it as best as possible.

The next box was a mess of flash drives. Different colors, shapes, some a little beaten, other looking shiny and new. There could be any number of files on them. He didn't envy Hughes, cataloging all of them. Daunting didn't begin to cover it.

The third box contained memory cards, the kind usually found in cameras. All the same size. Dozens of them. Raw footage maybe? From the same camera? Maybe what they used for their hidden cameras?

He studied the evidence before him. Had anyone already logged in any unchecked digital items left loose in the trailer? He didn't remember it, but it was possible he'd missed it in the list. One thing he did know about Brody, Whitney was special to him. Not the way anyone else used the word. It was why Brody kept returning to her, no matter how often she rejected him or how many times Rick scared the bastard away. To Brody, she was a possession he couldn't claim, no matter how hard he tried. Not even when he did his best to break her.

Brody would celebrate that attempt. Relive it as often as he could. Tell himself he'd won something that night. It wouldn't be with all these haphazardly kept files. It'd be somewhere…important. Somewhere close at hand.

His gaze went back to the box of burned discs. The empty case… Not an extra? He looked at the computer next to the box. God…

He slowly pulled the silver laptop closer. The dread in his gut now drew blood like blades. He lifted the lid and the machine automatically awakened. An unoriginal background image of a naked woman on her belly loaded onto the screen, fading somewhat as a password login popped up. Of course it did.

He frowned for a moment. Would Brody be dumb enough to use the same password he'd used at the station? It was worth a shot. He typed in the five digits that had once given this man the only real authority he'd ever had, his old badge number.

The password protection disappeared. Icon by icon, the

desktop loaded. Rick didn't care about any of them until the image of a disc finally came up, labeled only with an asterisk. He double clicked on it. He knew he shouldn't see this, if it was what he expected. Knew he didn't want to see it. But he had to know if this was the right one. He had to be sure.

The video viewer loaded, auto playing in full screen. Crystal clear, the picture showed him a familiar bed, back-dropped by the same blue and beige striped wallpaper he'd looked at only yesterday. The scene, however, was completely different from his silent memory.

A woman was being held down, her face shoved into the mattress by a man's large hand on the back of her head while he attacked her from behind. Rick didn't need to see her face. He knew those curls. Knew the silken caress of them twining through his fingers… Only to watch them being mercilessly yanked.

A horrible, strangled noise cut the air, startling him. Like the sound of someone's chest ripping open while they watched helplessly. Rick looked away, hands reflexively fisting on the edge of the box spring while that noise grew louder. He couldn't breathe, couldn't think. Could only hear that hoarse, enraged sound. It wasn't until he'd grabbed the night table beside Brody's bed, throwing it and the lamp atop it into the wall, that he realized the sound was coming from him.

Screaming. He was screaming. To the din of other men laughing. Taunting. Cheering and, God, grunting.

He fell back to the floor, his limbs turning to jelly, horror so real he couldn't get his throat muscles to swallow. To open at his command. He dropped his head to his knees, rearing back at the wetness he'd felt on his bare wrists. On his face.

Hot, he'd almost thought it was blood. It wasn't. They were tears. He wiped at them with his sleeves, gasping in a breath. Rational thought rushed back with a snap, but the pain in him at what he saw, the nausea and the rage, didn't fade in the slightest.

Little by little, he regained a thin control. The ordeal of what had been done to her kept going, but he didn't let himself look at the men. He stared at her. She didn't change, no matter how they struck her or yelled or demanded. She didn't change. She held herself together. Away from them. Never letting them have the satisfaction of getting more than they could force.

He hoped Brody saw that. Every time he watched this, Rick hoped Brody had seethed with impotent failure. The bastard hadn't beaten her. He hadn't broken or destroyed her. She was still standing. Brody was on a goddamn slab in a freezer. And so was the other worthless piece of shit who'd tried to take from her. But she was still standing, still fighting to find her own happiness.

Not willing to see any more, he dragged himself back to his knees, reaching for the built-in mousepad to turn the playback off. Right before he could, the camera shifted. What he'd assumed had been a tripod had apparently been someone else. Someone who handed the camera over to Dewar before smiling broadly into it.

Rick could only stare. "Who the fuck is that?"

Chapter Thirteen

Whitney's house was dark and silent when he got to the front door close to noon. He'd turned in the evidence to a stunned Hughes, who checked it in with a grim nod. Then, he'd ordered them all not to contact him if they didn't have to. Today, he needed to talk to Whitney. He needed to hold her and he needed to tell her what he'd found, what he'd done. What he still had to do.

Then he had to hope to God she forgave him.

Like his father had said, the shop was closed, but there seemed to be no one in Whitney's house, either. He opened the door, calling her name. Not even Alison answered. Given the hour, though, he realized she was probably at school. He would have thought, using the same logic, that Whitney was at the bakery, but her car was in the driveway. Then there was the fact that the door had been unlocked. He found the downstairs deserted. Creeping up the stairs, he kept all his senses alert, his hand over the butt of his service revolver, careful to skip that squeaking third step from the top. Finally, sound from the end of the hallway. The last room he expected to find her.

"Whitney?"

She sat on her knees on the floor, breathing in heavy gasps, her hair wild. A long and voluminous blue cotton nightgown hid all but her arms and her feet. He entered the room, shocked at the destruction. The bed, the mattress, blankets and pillows, all had been torn up. Shredded. Feathers and stuffing littered the floor, the wooden foot and headboards were destroyed, splintered, and hacked. Likely by the axe in her fisted hands. He circled widely, unwilling to startle her, especially with that weapon at the ready. "Whitney," he said again, softly, once he'd come around in front of her.

She stared at the destroyed bed in front of her, her face tear-stained and angry. "You shouldn't be here."

Yes, he should. He should always be where she needed him. "Will you let go of the axe?"

Her hands tightened around the handle.

"How about you tell me what's going on, then?" When she'd kissed him good-bye the night before, she'd been smiling. Teasing, even. "What brought all this on?"

She still wouldn't look at him. "They ruined me."

"No, honey, they didn't — "

"You *don't know!*" she snapped. "You don't know that I can barely sleep anymore. That every time I try, the dreams start and I'm right back there again. That I wake up screaming every day. I wake up *dying!*"

Chest constricting, all the knots in his throat threatened to choke him. He couldn't let it happen this time, though. Today, right now, he had to find a way to push the words out.

He had to give her what she needed.

He got down on the wooden floor with her, moving slowly as he covered her hands with his own. "I do know, Whit. You know I do."

It hurt, watching her try to hold all that pain and anger inside. Silent sobs shook her shoulders. He wanted to pull her against him, but the hands-off signals were screaming. He couldn't move his hands away. Hers were like ice but unless she said otherwise, he'd hold on.

"Last night meant the world to me," she whispered, licking her tears off her lips. "When nothing went wrong, I thought… I thought it'd be different. After. That *I'd* be different."

But reality didn't work that way.

"I felt that way, about coming home," he admitted.

She finally looked at him, thank God.

"I thought if I was home, back with my Dad, back where it was safe, I could leave it all behind. That I'd somehow be *me* again." He shook his head. "Instead, all it did was make me see how different I was from what I used to be. How much it hurt him not to know me anymore. But I didn't *want* him to know the things I'd seen. That I'd done. I didn't want him knowing any of it."

"You're better now than when you first came home."

He nodded. He wasn't fixed by any means. He doubted he'd ever be anything close to "normal" again. Once a bastard, always a bastard. But after years of her slowly and surely drawing him out, he'd improved. Found some stable ground for himself. Her quietly accepting ways, earning the trust he'd thought didn't exist, had changed him more than he would ever have believed. "I went to him today. We talked, we really talked. Because of you."

She shook her head. "Don't say that. It makes it sound like you're grateful."

He was, but he knew what she meant.

"All my life," she said softly, almost to herself. "I've taken care of people. I did what I had to do. What I was *supposed* to do. Never what I chose to. Now, when I finally have a chance to be even a little bit happy, to have something just for me… It's ruined. I can't even have the memory of it because all I can think about is what I *let* them do instead." She tugged on the axe, but he didn't let her move it. She struggled, but he didn't let go. She finally yelled at him, a brief roar of frustration.

"*Talk* to me, Whit." Just like him, she had to get it out. It would change nothing…and it would change everything. "No judgment, remember? Just an ear. Someone you know will hold your secrets. Someone you trust to help—"

"You can't help. I did this to myself." She let go, clapping her hands to her face and dragging the moisture off her cheeks angrily. "All of this is my own fault!"

"No, it's Brody's."

"Who the hell do you think let him in the door?"

He closed his mouth. She didn't want platitudes. But she sure as shit wasn't getting the axe back. He snatched it away, sliding it across the floor far from both their reach. She didn't even seem to care.

"When he first noticed me, it was easy to turn him down. Keep things light. Give him a smile and move away, on to the next customer. He got more aggressive, though, and it took me a long time to realize there was no one who'd stop him. The other deputies were useless. I refused to drag your father into it. And I had my mother to protect. He used to tell me how easy it would be to kill her and no one would ever know. Not even me.

"Sometimes, he'd be in my house, waiting for me to come home. Waiting in my bedroom. There was nowhere I could go to get away from him. I even tried to move, but I had to sell the bakery to do it and no one was interested. I was trapped here. With him. And the other people he worked for…" The threat of being thrown to Wheels of Pain had been real and terrifying. "They were so much worse and he made sure I knew it. If I gave him what he wanted, he'd protect us from them. Make sure Mom was never bothered. Never hurt. So I gave in. I let him do what he wanted. *I* did that. I let him make me into a whore because I was too much a coward to keep fighting."

"You are nobody's whore." He would never allow her—or anyone else—to believe that.

She gave a watery glance his way, though he couldn't say if she accepted his words or not. "When you came home, when you went into the station… God, I was so grateful for so many reasons. He was afraid of you and that made him bother me so much less. But when he did come, I still couldn't tell him no. Whenever I tried, and you have to believe I tried, he hurt my mother. Later, he'd hurt Alison. I wanted to be braver. I wanted to be smarter. But I was weak and I was scared."

And she hadn't wanted him to know. To help her. If he had, Rick knew from the experience of trying to help Shana, the punishment was almost always crippling. Wheels of Pain had too strong a grip on their county, the corruption and violence more than one man could take down alone. It had taken four people — all of them nearly dying for it — the state police and the fucking FBI, to break the grip that gang had. In the meantime, people suffered. *She'd* suffered. There was more than she was saying, he sensed her still holding back, but he wasn't there to push. All he could do was listen and let her know he wasn't going anywhere, no matter what she revealed.

"They were already here when I came home that night. All three of them. Smiling at me. I still see those smiles when I close my eyes at night." Her lips trembled and she took a deep breath. "Mom was terrified and Alison's lip had already been split. Brody made me an offer. They'd leave the others alone, as long as I did what they said, all night long. Whatever they said. Otherwise, it would be all of us. So I did it. I locked them both in Mom's room and I did what I had to."

And hated herself ever after.

"That's when you came for the gun."

She nodded. "I couldn't let it happen again. I knew he'd never stop unless I *made* him stop. It took me too long to see that he'd keep taking and taking and taking. Appeasing him did nothing. He had to know I meant it.

"When he came back, he thought he had me right where he wanted me. That I'd *finally figured it out*." The way she lowered her voice, it was obviously a quote. "He never saw the gun coming. Not until it was between his eyes."

Except that wasn't where she'd shot him.

"I ordered him off my porch. He tried to charge me. The only reason he didn't die then is because my hand was shaking. But it was close enough. He didn't come back after that. None of them did. But they didn't have to. The nightmares do what he never could." The misery in her eyes, huge tears spilling over her cheeks… "You know the fucking tragedy of it all? My mother died two months later in her sleep, anyway. All those years, caring for her, protecting her, holding on to her… For nothing. She never knew who I was again. Never knew the danger she'd ever been in. Never knew anything at all."

"Not nothing," he corrected, his voice feeling like gravel. "She was safe. Even when she wasn't, she didn't know it. It might be small comfort—"

"Very small."

"But it's something. Something for *you* to hold on to." The same way he'd held on to the fact that Cade made it back home. To an eventual wife. To an eventual *life*.

"What if I'm always like this?" A very real fear in her voice. "How am I supposed to spend the rest of my life? Afraid of everything?"

"You're not afraid of me." Not even remotely.

She gave a wet, almost bitter, laugh. "Oh Rick, you have *no* idea. You scare me more than anything in the world." But she smiled as she said it. Just enough to take the sting out of her words. Because he knew exactly what she meant.

He rubbed his thumb over her cheek, wiping away the tears again. "You terrify me, too, honey."

She laughed again, her face crumpling as she turned into his hand and sobbed. "You don't need this mess in your life. You really don't."

But he wanted it. Wanted *her*. "I'm not letting you push me away, so don't bother trying. If you can't get past this, we'll get help. Whatever you need, we'll do it."

"We?" She knew he hated therapists and it showed

clearly on her face.

"Yes, *we.*"

Poor thing, she looked genuinely confused. "Why? Why won't you let me—"

"Because you didn't let me do it to you." She'd loved him and nothing he'd done had shaken her from it. He came to rely on it. He needed it now. He'd always needed it, he'd just been too blind to see. When he came home, he'd been too broken to face a truth that had always been a part of his life. Even now, he wasn't sure he could ever tell her what she deserved to know. All he could do was pull her into his arms and say the only thing he could strangle out. The only thing he'd ever been able to tell her and hope like hell she understood one more time. "*Whitney.*"

She froze, every part of her stiff and unyielding. Then, suddenly, her arms slipped under his coat, wrapping tight around him, and she sighed. Finally relaxing. He would have relaxed too, if her movement wasn't shoving something hard in his pocket into his side. Shit. He'd almost forgotten what he'd come here for. He held on still, not wanting to let go. But there couldn't be any more secrets—especially not this one.

"Whit," Damn, his voice sounded rough. She stiffened immediately in response. "We have more we have to deal with."

She sagged. "Do we really have to?" He didn't answer and she sighed again, this time far more reluctantly, pulling herself back into a sitting position. "What now?"

He tugged on the object in his pocket, which was as loathe to be removed as he was to show it to her. "Before you see this, I have to ask something. The third man. Why didn't you tell me about him? About any of this?"

It took several careful swallows before she could speak. "Because I never wanted you to…hate yourself for what I…" She struggled to keep her composure. "You would have killed them. I couldn't put more blood on your hands. Not for me. Not for my cowardice."

He wanted to say she was wrong, but she wasn't. He'd have hunted all three of them down. This third man…he still might. "Did you know him?"

She shook her head. "They called him Dan. I'd never seen him before and I haven't since."

There was something there. Something familiar, but his brain wasn't connecting to it. If Gorski knew who the bastard was, he was in danger. Or hell, given the money from the site and the videos, there was a chance this third man was another bloody suspect. This whole mess was a frustrating circle of greed and cruelty and silence. There was no way to know which end was up. The disc finally came out and, hesitantly, he handed it to her.

"What is this?"

"It's a DVD I found in Brody's trailer."

She just looked at him, still not understanding.

"Brody and Dewar, maybe this Dan person—" God, how could he tell her the rest?

"Rick," she said sternly. "What the hell is this?"

"It's you."

"Me? Me wh—" Understanding flashed in her eyes, followed by a revulsion so strong the case clattered to the floor and he thought she might be sick right there. "Oh, God," she groaned, backing away. Repeating it over and over.

"It's okay, no one else is ever going to see it. We'll

destroy it."

"Else?" she whispered, then she pinned him with a horrified gaze. "*You've* seen that?"

"Whit—" He didn't even know what he wanted to say. Only that he needed her to stop looking at him like that.

"You…you…" Whatever she might have said disappeared when she clapped her hand to her mouth and scrambled toward the bathroom connected to her bedroom. He followed, helping her get there on legs that didn't seem able to hold her. She shook in his arms long after her body stopped its fruitless spasms.

He yanked the hand towel from the sink rack and pushed it into her hand. She took it, wiping her face listlessly, saying nothing. She didn't move after that, just lay against him. Worn out. Shattered.

"What I saw doesn't change anything," he murmured, smoothing her hair back from her face. "It doesn't change that you're still the bravest, strongest person I know."

She didn't respond. Didn't even seem to be breathing.

"It doesn't change how proud of you I am."

"No one's proud here," she replied hoarsely.

"Yes. I am." He jostled her, the tightness in his chest loosening a little when she pushed at his arm angrily. *That's my girl.* She didn't know it, but she was a bigger fighter than he'd ever been. Probably why he'd never stood a chance against her. "You've been through hell and back, Whitney Jean, and you came out of it with your soul intact. Still brave enough to keep risking everything for the people you love. How could I not be proud of you? Why aren't you proud of yourself?"

"Because I didn't risk what you think." She shook her

head. "I just thought… I *had* to believe the best in people. Don't you see? If there's something good in everyone, maybe there was still something good in *me*. Something I didn't use up, resenting how alone I was. How angry and bitter I felt. I'm not brave. I'm the worst kind of coward."

"No, honey. You're human." Wonderfully, beautifully human. "It would take a saint to go through what you have without getting angry. Most people don't do anything positive with it like you have."

She leaned back into him, rubbing her head against his shoulder. "*You* did."

Well… Shit. He'd never thought of it that way. "I guess we're two of a kind, then."

Her hand settled on his leg, holding on. A few minutes later, "Rick?" Something in her tone had his ears prickling. "You said you found that thing in Brody's trailer."

"Mm-hmm." He kept petting her hair. It was odd to be comfortable, wedged together on the floor of the small bathroom, but he was.

"Why were you searching his trailer?"

Damn it.

"And wouldn't anything you found there be *evidence*?"

"I'm not sure we should get into this right now. You've already had some shocks."

Her hand clamped on his thigh with a surprising amount of strength. "What did you *do*?"

No point in lying. "I'm protecting you."

"By stealing evidence and impeding your own murder investigation?" She sat up, turning to look at him, her puffy eyes narrowed. "By going back on *everything* you believe in?"

In a word? Yes. "You didn't kill Brody or Jason. All that disc will do is give them a reason to tighten the investigation further on you. I'm not letting that happen."

"*Further?*"

He bit back the expletives. "Cade wants me to bring you in for questioning. Probably booking."

"Boo—" She jolted into a sitting position, clearly doing some fast thinking of her own about his plans. "Do you really think I'm going to let you throw away everything you've built here? Are you insane?"

Yeah, he kind of was. No price was too high when it came to her. Not for him.

"I'm not letting you do this." She got to her feet and stepped over him, heading back into the room to pick that vile thing up.

It took precious seconds to get back up, to follow her, seconds she used well. She already had it in hand, heading to the stairs. One quick yank as she tried to pass him and he'd snatched the case from her hands. "It's already too late."

She spun, grabbing for it. "No, it's not. Cade will understand."

"They don't need this to make the case." Not against Wainwright. And since she'd never filed a report, never had a rape kit done, they wouldn't have one against the third assailant, even if they did find him. A video wasn't enough these days, not by a long shot.

"It's enough to make a case against *you*."

Yes, it was. He popped the disc from the case and promptly bent it in half. It snapped loudly in the silence. Twice more when he broke each half a second time. Then, he flung the pieces into the mess by the bed. Four more destroyed shards of that night. Turning to face her, he looked at her, waiting for her to say something, anything, about what was wrong or right.

She looked down, hands on her hips. Said nothing.

"You *didn't* kill those bastards."

She looked up, lips tight. Still nothing.

"If you had, I'd still have done the same damn thing." Without blinking.

"Even if it makes you just as corrupt as the people you threw out of your department?" A soft question, but no less meaningful for it.

"I can live with it."

"Can you?" Her strong facade crumpled, heartache taking over. "Because I can't."

He sucked in a breath. He'd heard those words before from others. Knew too well the danger of them. "Don't say things like that."

"Like the truth? God forbid we should have any of that." She dragged both hands through her hair as if she wanted to scream. "You never listen. Not once, you've never listened."

He stayed absolutely still, frightened by the flatness of her voice. "Listened to what?"

"To *me*." A scathing glare. "You *cannot* protect me, Rick. Not like this. You can't take away what I've done or what's happened because it makes you feel better. You can't keep taking the brunt and leave me with the blame."

"I have never blamed you—"

"*I* blamed me!" It was almost a scream. "Every time you jumped into the fray, every time you got hurt for me or had to pull me out of trouble, I blamed me. Now this? No. I won't be the reason you lose the one thing about yourself you believe is good. Not for my sake."

"Haven't you figured it out, Whit?" He took a careful step closer, glad when she didn't step back. Didn't flinch when he held her face in both hands.

She shook her head. "I won't be the reason you can't look in the mirror."

That's why he trusted her. Why he always would. He leaned down, watching her all the way, to press a soft kiss to her forehead, his arm wrapping around her shoulders to pull her into him. "You're the only reason I can."

Her body didn't soften against him and he realized he wasn't getting through to her. Worse, he had the unwelcome sense she was getting her point across to him. "We can—" They both jumped at the sound of his phone ringing in his pocket. Fuck. "I have to take it."

She pushed away, wrapping her arms around herself. "Go."

There was no forgiveness in her tone. Nothing to tell him what she was thinking at all. Just the absolute order for him to leave. He almost ignored it, unwilling to let her shut him out. To ignore what he'd been trying to tell her since he got there, but she turned from him. Shut him out. Again.

He answered the call while moving down the hall to the stairs, so she wouldn't overhear. "This better be important."

"We found Gorski, sir." Hughes, sounding grimly excited.

"Where?" He kept going, hitting the first floor, past the living room and into the less echoing dining room.

"New Jersey."

Rick's heart stuttered. "Excuse me?"

"New Jersey, sir. I followed a hunch, tracked down Gorski's older daughter. Turns out she saw her father in a news story about the trial, saw how messed up he was. She came home a month ago. Took him back with her to dry him out and take care of him. He's been across the country all this time, sir."

"Then who the hell shot Brody?"

"That's why I'm calling, sir. There's been another shooting. About twenty minutes ago. Victim was a twenty to twenty-five-year-old male, shot in the chest multiple times in the middle of President's Park."

Rick heard a quiet snick behind him, telling him he wasn't alone.

"Witnesses say the perpetrator was a petite blonde woman—"

He turned, already damning himself for making such a massive, stupid mistake, but all he saw was a flash of blonde curls and silver before a loud report turned the whole world to nothing.

Chapter Fourteen

Whitney's scream was still echoing in her ears as she stared at the blood on her hands. Rick's blood. On her fingers, on her floor. He lay so still, but she could see the blood in his hair, where the skin seemed torn, on his jacket. On the ground. Oh, God, the blood—

A stinging slap spun her back, knocking her off her knees.

"Shut! Up!"

Dazed, Whitney looked up, blinking in confusion at the person pointing a gun at her. "*Alison?*"

"You *called* him?" Alison's gun hand shook so hard, Whitney expected her to drop the small silver weapon. "Everything I've done for you and you called *him*?"

Ignoring her niece, ignoring the gun, she reached under his coat collar, searching desperately for a pulse. She found it with shaking fingertips. Still strong. But for how long? With a brutal chill, she realized she couldn't let Alison know he was alive. She dropped her head over his shoulders, hoping her relief could pass for grief. Alison wasn't good at understanding other people's emotions on her best day. She could only hope that sad fact held true this time as well. She needed the next few seconds to try to get her head together.

She'd already been coming down the stairs after Rick when she heard the gun go off. Her heart stopped as she'd fallen to her knees next to him. She still wasn't sure if it had started again or not. Alison stood, weapon extended, wearing one of Whitney's own dresses under a tan overcoat. A coat spattered with…blood? As was the dress. And her face. Fine speckles dotted her neck, chin, and cheeks. There was too much for it to be Rick's… Wasn't there?

"Why?" It was all she could push out of her constricting throat. Why would she do this?

"*Why?*" Alison's disdain was palpable, twisting her features into a mask of hate. "Because no matter what I do, all you ever want is *him!*" Alison swung the gun, kicking Rick's side viciously over and over. "I've done *everything* for you! But it's never enough. *Never!*"

"Alison, stop!" Whitney stood up, pushing them both away from his inert body, shoving Alison onto the dining room table, reaching for her hands. For the gun. She came to sudden stillness when Alison kept a tight grip, pointing the weapon right in her face. Close enough to feel the heat still warming the barrel.

"Get off me." Cold. How had she never noticed how cold Alison's eyes were?

Whitney backed away, hands up and shaking, but she stopped when her heels bumped into Rick's legs. "Wh-what are you doing?"

"I'm finishing this," the girl answered breathlessly. She smiled, unsteadily, then wider. As if she were somehow enjoying the moment. God, Whitney realized with dawning horror. Alison actually *was*. "Get those cuffs off his belt. Put them on, hurry up."

Whitney kneeled, only glancing to where Rick's handcuffs peeked out from beneath the hem of his coat. Her fingers fumbled with the latch on his heavy belt, but she didn't dare take her eyes off Alison for longer than it took to blink. The cuffs tore free and she fit one over her own wrist. The other wasn't as easy, but they finally clicked and locked into place.

"You're exactly like my mother," Alison accused. "No matter how much I took care of her, it wasn't enough, either."

"It *is* enough, Alison." Whitney raised her bound hands, palms out. *Get her away from him. Give him a chance…* "I'm sorry, you just…surprised me."

Alison's tirade stopped, but she seemed waiting for more.

Whitney tried to make her mind work. "Wh-what did you do?"

The utter lack of expression on the girl's face was terrifying. "Come on. I'll show you." Alison gestured with the gun toward the swinging kitchen door. Did she intend to make them go out the back?

She pushed to her feet, leading the way into the kitchen, almost relieved when Alison kept the gun trained on her. She kept on through the kitchen, stopping only to slip on a pair of shoes. Once outside, she had no idea where to head. The garage, where Alison did her painting?

"That way." Alison pointed to the trees. Whitney hesitated, a mistake because Alison shoved at her back. "Go."

Nodding, she made herself move, but dread cloaked her along with the shadows from the leafy canopy. No one would know they were in there. Not with enough time to help. Places to hide weren't easy to find, not with the open space between the big elms, oaks, and boulders. Dried leaves and twigs littered the ground, revealing every step anyone took. At the very least, *her* steps. The crunching and snagging of the overgrowth catching on her nightgown gave every movement away. Especially when Alison pushed her on a trail only she seemed to know.

"Why is there blood on you?" Whitney tried to keep her voice calm. "Are you hurt?"

"No one hurts me, Aunt Whitney. You know that."

She did, actually. Alison had said as much after her fight with the Reed girl. She'd said it that day with the same deadly clarity. No one would ever hurt her again. Not without regretting it. "Whose gun is that?" Hers didn't have that black grip.

"Brody's." So matter of fact. As if that wasn't the most incriminating thing she'd ever said. "Your bullets, though."

"My what?" She turned, shocked, but Alison just pushed her forward again.

"Brody only had six in his gun that night. I used the ones you hid around the house in case Brody came back. Seemed fitting, don't you think?"

"Fitting for what? And what do you mean *that night*?" But she knew. Feeling sick again, Whitney stumbled, pausing to put her shackled hands on the nearest tree. Even with the gun behind her back, all she could see was the look on Alison's face the year before, shoved into the recliner. Her lip bleeding, murder in her eyes as she'd glared at Brody.

"You're the one who killed him."

"Of course I did."

Whitney closed her eyes at that remorseless acknowledgement.

"I killed them all." Alison pulled at Whitney's shoulder,
no trace of gentleness in her touch now. The message was
clear—keep moving. "You were afraid. I know what that's
like, knowing they'll come back. That you won't be able to
stop them next time. You needed to know they wouldn't. No
one is ever coming again. Not for us."

Whitney couldn't have said another word if she wanted
to. Her throat was squeezing so tight it had turned into a
vise. She walked numbly for a long while, starting to see the
faint trail in the dirt, where the branches of the wild shrubs
were already broken, the small rocks cleared. This was where
Alison had been spending her time?

The trail opened into a clearing, surrounded by rocks.
Pieces of wood—dead trees, maybe?—formed a semi-circle
in the middle. All around, Whitney saw melted candles, paint
on rocks, and finally, in one corner, the hallmarks of Alison's
life…books. A neat shelf of them, hidden in a small alcove
she'd created between two boulders. There was more there,
too, beneath the shelf. Small items, trinkets or something. Or
were they keepsakes?

"Where are we?"

"My safe place." Alison pointed out where she expected
Whitney to sit. When she did, Alison came down next to her,
leaning close and looking at Whitney with the intense study
she usually used on one of her drawings. "You're the only
one I'd ever trust enough to bring here."

Oh. Whitney blinked, trying to process the swings in

Alison's moods. This time, she knew, her life depended on it. Rick's too. "I…I thought you were angry at me."

"I was," Alison replied dismissively. "But I realized you just didn't know everything. Rick doesn't tell you much about his work, does he?"

It was meant to be a dig, but Whitney had to admit, it was the truth. Of course, she hadn't asked. She hadn't *wanted* to know anything about Brody's murder investigation.

"My mother never listened to me. Never cared about the reasons I did anything." Alison's dark eyes were so fixed on her, Whitney had to fight not to recoil. "Not like you. You've always listened. Reasons mean everything to you, even when you think I did something wrong."

Whitney nodded, willing to do anything to keep Alison talking, to buy time.

"Vera wasn't like that at all. She didn't care that her boyfriend was after me, that he kept coming to my room. All she cared about was her drugs and him. When I cut him, she didn't listen. She just got rid of me."

"You *cut* him?" Of course Vera wouldn't mention that. Not that she'd stopped the car long enough for Alison to do more than get her bags from the backseat.

"Did you know it only takes two minutes, at *most*, to die from a sliced artery? Less than a minute if it's the carotid."

Whitney shook her head again. God, how had she never seen this side of her niece before? Or had she? Had she simply thought a child couldn't be this dangerous? This unfeeling? Rick had known. Rick had known there was something wrong with Alison, but even he couldn't have realized… "Did you kill that man too?"

"No, I missed the artery." For that, Alison seemed to

have genuine regret. "But it scared him. And every time he looks in the mirror, for the rest of his life, he'll remember me. Remember how close I got." There was a strange light in her eyes as she spoke. The same one that had been there as she'd held the gun over Rick in the dining room. "Vera never put me first. Not like you. You loved me. You always protected me, even when they hurt you."

All Whitney could do was shudder, bowing her head. No matter what she did, how she tried to avoid dealing with it, everything always came back to that night.

"My mother would never have done that for me. Your mother wouldn't have, either."

"Yes, she would," Whitney whispered. "You didn't know her. Not the real her. My mother gave everything for me. Every day that she could." It was a truth she'd almost forgotten over the many years of caring for a woman who had become a confused stranger. Carrie had raised her alone and fought tooth and nail to give her a home. To give her a happy life for as long as she'd been able.

"She was weak," Alison replied, the decree so blank it stunned. "I fed her, I watched her. Listened to her sing to herself and talk about nothing for hours. Day after day, I tried to figure out why you kept her around. Why you held on so tight. All she did was get in your way. Hold you back. Give Brody a way to control you. She had no redeeming value at all."

"She did to *me*."

Alison shrugged, bored. "She was better off dead."

Unwise or not, Whitney's temper rose. "Stop, Alison."

"It's the truth. She didn't even fight me when I put the pillow over her face."

The crack of her hand over Alison's cheek rocked the girl's head back. But that was the only reaction it got.

"You were happier without her. Just like you were happier without Brody. *I* did that for you."

"You did *not* do that!" Anger, grief, frustration, feelings she couldn't name coursed through her. All of them useless, because in her soul, she knew Alison wasn't lying. This wasn't some sick fantasy. She'd *killed* people. Killed them without compunction. "She was *helpless…*"

"Brody wasn't." Alison's cheek glowed a brilliant red. "He was the real monster. I started following him, after I saw him driving by the house. Did you know he did that? That he was still watching you? Looking for a way to get back at you?"

No, she hadn't. Not that Alison was the best source for the truth, but she'd known, in the back of her mind, that Brody would never stop being a threat.

"I used to sneak into his trailer. Go through his things. It was so easy to mess with his head. Make him think he was losing things, that he was messing up. But he wasn't going away, so I had to think of something else. That's when I went through his computer.

"You weren't the only one he watched. Or the only one he attacked. He'd drug girls all the time. Him and his friends. They'd film 'em and put 'em up on his website. He was a pig and he deserved to bleed like one."

"Alison, how did Brody die?"

"I followed him to the bar, like I usually did on Fridays. He saw me trying to get in. A mistake, I admit." She said it the way one would regret a bad haircut. "He dragged me down the alley to the back parking lot. I'm not sure how, but he figured out that I'm the one who'd been getting into his trailer on the way. Two and two, I guess, because of what I took. You and I were the only ones who'd want that."

She pulled out one of her books from the shelf, letting the pages fall open. She lifted a small plastic rectangle with her spare hand. She brought it to Whitney, putting it in her palm the way a pet would bring a gift to her master, complete with the expectant expression. A memory stick, marked with a small silver asterisk. Just like the DVD. *Oh God...*

"He was so busy choking me he didn't notice me pulling the gun from his side until the first shot." The girl's face was all flushed with color now. Not embarrassment, like Whitney's would. Excitement. "When he fell, I ran—of course I ran—but for the first time in my life I knew what it was like to be happy. Really, truly happy." Alison's smile would have been beautiful if it weren't utterly disturbing. "I'm the one who decides now. Decides who lives, who dies, who hurts the most. No one is ever going to decide for me ever again."

Whitney watched her, her heart breaking. She'd tried so hard to help this girl. To give her a safe, happy home, show her she could be part of a family. All along, she'd been broken. Destroyed beyond repair.

"After Brody, Jason was easy. He trolls for girls all the time. I just had to play along. He didn't even remember me, can you believe it? Some makeup, some slutty clothes, and I could have been anyone to him."

Whitney didn't want to hear the details. Couldn't bear it. "What about the blood on you now?"

Alison sighed. "I found Dan. In Brody's phone. Danny Wainwright was in his contacts list." She picked up another item from the mishmash of things below the shelf. There was a frightening number of things there, mixed with dried flowers and melted candles. She stroked the glass surface of it almost lovingly, her fingers squeezing the rubberized outer case tightly. "Turns out he works for a guy Brody knew. A guy he owed a lot of money to. Someone else he was screwing, I guess. His text messages were really pissed.

"He wasn't hard to get out here. I told him I had proof he stole from his boss, but if he gave me enough money, I'd give it to him. After this morning, I knew you needed them all to die. So you could stop being so afraid. Now you can."

God, oh God... Such childish logic. So glacial and sure. How did you reason with that? *Make her feel safe. Keep her calm. Look for a way out.* She looked down at the memory card still in her hand. She curled it in her fist and took the biggest risk of her life. "Thank you."

Alison stilled.

"I needed you and you did what had to be done." It was what Alison wanted. For Whitney to need her. To want her, rely on her. A simple need, twisted into a possessiveness so clear now that Whitney ached at not having seen it before.

"Of course," Alison replied solemnly, slipping easily back into the understanding guise she'd worn that morning. Nurturing Alison mode. Like a mask she could put on at will. Now that Whitney had seen the terrifying absolutist beneath, though, only the falseness came through. "That's why I brought you here. So we don't have to be apart anymore. We don't have to be scared of anyone taking either of us away. No one will ever come between us again." She leaned in, hugging Whitney with one arm, pressing her cheek to Whitney's. "I dressed like you, used your bullets, so they'd know we did this together. So they'd know to come find us."

Confused, Whitney shivered, knowing something horrible was about to happen, unsure what it could be. Then Alison's hand came up, the muzzle of the small gun pressing against Whitney's temple.

"*We* decide now." Alison whispered reverently, pushing the gun harder.

All at once, Whitney realized what she meant to do. Time had run out and panic was all that was left. She shoved as hard as she could, sending Alison to the ground, the gun falling out of her hand. Standing, Whitney almost jumped for the weapon, but Alison was closer. There wasn't time. She spun and ran, crashing through bushes to the open trees. She screamed when a shot rang out, hitting a trunk she just passed. Hands still bound, she ran, trying to avoid a straight path. Two more shots, only one close to her. Moving targets were harder to hit, Rick had said, especially ones moving erratically. The important thing was to get as far from where Alison seemed to be standing to fire. Back to the house. Back to help Rick before Alison could catch up to her…

They hadn't walked more than half a mile away from the house, but to Whitney, that distance seemed insurmountable. She ran from one large tree to another, knowing her breathing was too loud and her steps were crashing through the woods. She couldn't help either, but she paused, trying to listen past her own heartbeat thundering in her ears. No other sounds, but she didn't let that fool her.

She sprinted again, passing a boulder only to be yanked back, a hand fitting over her mouth. She knew that hand and almost started to cry in relief at the feel of it. Instead, she turned into him, burying her face against his chest. "You're *alive*."

"Mostly," Rick agreed gruffly. He pulled her back, holding her face with both hands to look at her carefully. "Are *you* okay?"

No. Not at all. But he was here and miraculously, so was she. He dug into one of the pockets on his belt, pulling out the small silver keys to the handcuffs. He bent his head to fit it into the lock, swaying as he did. She looked at the vicious wound gouged through the hair on the side of his head, bleeding freely down his neck…and down the right side of his shirt. She could see where it soaked the shoulder of his uniform, was starting to spill down the back too. Once the cuffs were off, she realized his eyes were unfocused. "You're not."

He blinked slowly, his mouth flattening into a hard line. "No, I'm not. But I'm good enough." They both started at the distant sounds of sirens. Still too far to be of much use, but definitely coming closer. "We're a quarter mile out." He pointed through the tree line. "Stay in this direction. Get to my Dad's house. You can get to Cade together from there."

She caught his intention right away. "You're coming with me."

"No, I'm tracking that bitch down. *You're* getting somewhere safe." He knelt, keeping his head and neck rigidly straight, but she could see the movement cost him. He pulled a snub-nosed revolver from his ankle holster. "Take this and run."

"I'm not leaving you like this."

"Goddamn it, Whit!" She almost felt better at his familiar curse, despite the fact that it was an exasperated whisper. "We're not fighting about this now."

"Then when? After you get yourself killed because you

can't even turn your head?" To say nothing of the blood loss. His shirt was more soaked down the back than she'd realized. "You're going to pass out again any second."

"Head wounds always bleed more." He glared, but it lost meaning when he was this waxy. "Cade is coming for you."

"She's killed four people, Rick. And she's suicidal. You're in no shape—"

He yanked her toward him, quieting her with a hard kiss. "I love you."

She gaped up at him.

"I should have said it before. Should have figured it out a long time ago. I was wrong to let you think—"

Her fingers covered his mouth. "Not like this. Not like a good-bye."

"Then get your ass to my dad's. Tell Cade and the others where I am and stay with Dad. I'm not fast right now. It's better if I defend the path from here."

She struggled with the logical sense he was making. It went against everything she felt, to leave him bleeding and impaired. But he hadn't survived two different kinds of wars being stupid. She nodded, kissed him one more time, and did what he commanded.

She ran.

Chapter Fifteen

Rick tried to bring his vision together, but between the pounding in his skull and the blackness creeping in around the edges, seeing double was the least of his problems. Blindsided by a damned teenager. He fucking knew better, but here he was, bleeding and possibly about to die because of it. At *fucking* home.

He waited until the pale blue of Whitney's nightgown disappeared. The last thing he wanted her to see was what was going to happen in these woods. It was either him or the girl. He didn't think both of them could possibly come out of this alive without a miracle and he may have already used his store of those.

He looked around, not sure where Alison might be by now. She would be able to hear the sirens as well as he, would know the sheriffs were coming. The smart thing would have been to stay where he'd awakened on the dining room floor and wait for Cade and the others to arrive, but he couldn't be smart this time. He'd heard Whitney fighting for him. Heard the back door slam, though he'd been unable to do anything about either. Ears ringing, brain throbbing, heart pumping so hard he felt like he'd been running for miles, he'd struggled to follow them. He simply hadn't been able to leave her to Alison's mercies.

Thankfully, there was no mistaking Whitney's trail. When the report of those shots echoed through the trees, he'd felt the worst terror of his life. Every part of him had locked, clenching in refusal. Then came the crashing, Whitney running right toward him. She was alive. Nothing else mattered but keeping her that way. Not his pride. Not even his fears that he might not see her again.

He made his way to the closest large tree, both hands holding his Remington. Two concerns remained now that Whitney was safe. She'd need at least seven minutes to get to the house. Fifteen to bring reinforcements. No way in hell could he let her psychotic niece pass him.

Arrowing his senses past the pain, past the cold taking hold all over him, he listened again. Only silence greeted him. Too many people had come through, the insects and the animals had yet to return to their normal sounds. He shifted to another tree, cursing inwardly when the earth seemed to spin, nearly going dark before he could get his bearings. Weakness numbed his fingers, making his legs shake as well.

Another loud report, a chunk of the tree behind him exploding, forcing him to run to another for slim cover. Her fifth shot. Her weapon maxed out at twelve. Still enough in there for her to end his life.

Firing once behind him in the general direction of the shots, he pushed off for the next tree. She discharged again, causing another redirect. He faced the tree this time, swearing as he tried to spot her from the edge. Six shots. Four minutes for Whitney. There Alison was, the tan of her coat peeking out from behind another tree. He squeezed off a shot, his 1911 R1 blowing a whole chunk out of the wood, the sound of it blasting through his head. The jacket fell.

"*Goddamn it!*" Smart. She was always smart. He turned to put his back to the tree and came face to face with his enemy for the last time.

She watched him with those empty dark eyes, far enough out of his reach that she could easily pull the trigger before he even lifted his weapon. Her gaze fixed dispassionately on his wound. "That looks like it hurts."

At least she didn't gloat.

"Just my pride." He had to guess the pain in his ribs was thanks to her, too. He didn't care much, he was used to pain. The damn blood loss was making his head light, though. His body shook and that pissed him off. The added insult of dying at the hands of a little girl with a glorified BB gun? Yeah, that one would follow him into eternity.

"Your friends are coming, right?"

"You have some time." Not much, but some. Which she already knew. "You won't get out of these woods alive." But she knew that too.

As expected, she accepted that with a disinterested flicker of her lashes. He thought as much, since Hughes said she'd left witnesses. It explained her wearing Whitney's clothes, too. She'd wanted to lead them here. Probably hoping *he'd* be the one to find them. One last *fuck you* from the grave. The current situation might work for her, too. Any end that meant he and Whitney weren't together would be good enough for her.

He hated the thought that she'd get anything she wanted out of this. The worst part was, knowing Whitney, she'd blame herself if he didn't come back. She'd be alone and destroyed, all over again. Punishment for not loving Alison *enough*.

Alison's gaze suddenly switched from side to side, as if she was hearing something. Damn it, his hearing was off. There it was, a crackle. His vision might be compromised, but he still caught the flash of light blue behind a tree, ten yards away. Son of a bitch, she'd come back. If they got out of this alive, he was going to kill her. Alison took a step back, which was all he needed.

"Ah-ah-ah." He clicked his tongue, nudging the nose of his now pointed gun. "Move again and my trigger finger gets itchy." Now probably wasn't the best time for a standoff, but he couldn't aim well enough to end this with one shot. It wasn't one he could hold for long, either. Maybe, just maybe, he could hold out long enough. "You're under arrest, Alison, for the murders of Brody Roberts, Jason Dewar, and whoever the hell that last bastard was."

"They don't matter." Her voice, flat and low, set off that prickling at the back of his neck. "None of you ever did."

No, he figured they didn't. Not to her. The only person who meant a damn to her had run away. And was currently behind her, holding the gun he gave her to the back of Alison's head.

"We matter to Whitney."

"She's better without you."

Probably. God knew he didn't deserve Whitney's love or devotion. But she chose him. Right now, she was risking everything to protect him, damn her. Angry as he was, that meant everything to him. "She didn't run from me, though, did she?"

"She didn't understand, that's all."

"That you meant to kill her?" His own panting sounded rough in his ears, the dark hedging in closer to his vision. So cold now, though his heart seemed to be racing. His teeth began to chatter.

"She's *mine*. She belongs with me."

"She deserves a life of her own." His tongue felt thick in his mouth, slurring his words. Time. Not enough time.

"You'll never find out what she deserves, will you?" All the hate she'd ever had for him was clear in the twisted smile on her face. "A couple more minutes and you'll bleed out, so it won't matter what you think. Until then, I can just watch you die slowly, knowing I'm the last thing you'll ever see. That alone makes it all worth it."

They both heard Whitney cock the revolver. "Put it down, Alison."

The girl shook her head, not at all surprised at the situation she was in. It bothered him that her expression didn't change. He tried to figure out why, but he was losing his grip and that seemed far more important.

"I won't go back." Alison looked right at him, a message in her eyes he couldn't understand. "I'll never go back there."

"Please," Whitney begged.

"No." Resolute. Alison raised her gun, pointing it right at his heart. She'd waited until his strength had faded, his arm too sluggish to respond. His vision swayed to the side, but he still stared at that smile. That terrible, macabre expression of happiness. It looked so wrong on her. Suddenly, it was so clear, as if she'd said her intentions right in his ear. She was pushing Whitney for a reason. Alison lifted her arm higher, her finger squeezing the trigger.

Any future that would keep him and Whitney apart...

"Whit, no—"

But the gun went off and it was too late. Alison fell, leaving Whitney standing there, agony on her stricken face. Slowly, so slow he wasn't sure if it was the blood loss or reality, but she sank to her knees, already reaching for him. He didn't realize he'd fallen until she lifted him, his head resting on her lap while she started screaming for help.

He thought she was screaming, anyway. Her voice was sounding very far away.

"My dad," he tried to say, but his lips were numb. Richard would take care of her.

She looked down at him, shaking her head, maybe even shaking him. He couldn't tell. It didn't matter. She was here. She was safe. She looked into his eyes, the most beautiful thing he'd ever known. The light above the trees lit her hair, haloing it with brilliant gold. He wanted to tell her it was okay, that he was fine, but the light was getting brighter. Too bright to keep his eyes open. He fought it to keep looking at her. Just a little longer...

Too soon, the light was all there was.

• • •

Whitney sat in the chair beside Rick's hospital bed, willing him to wake up. The bandage on the side of his head hid most of the damage, but she only had to close her eyes to remember it. To remember him falling unconscious in her arms. The gash had taken twenty-eight stitches to close and he'd required an emergency blood transfusion. Something they'd achieved quickly only because his father had heard the shots and come running despite all the commands from deputies trying to keep him back. That and the clinic supplies kept in his garage. Which was why the man sitting next to her had a bandage of his own on his arm, along with a pack of half-eaten cookies and a large bottle of juice on the bedside table.

Across the bed, on the other side of Rick's feet, sat the she-devil card shark who was currently besting Rick's father at poker with almost ridiculous ease. He blamed the blood donation, but Whitney knew it was more that Richard couldn't quite concentrate. Katrina kept him playing, though, and the distraction was welcome to everyone in the room.

"Just admit it," Richard complained in his own good-natured way. "Poker was part of your training in Langley, wasn't it?"

Katrina laughed softly. "Nope. My uncle insisted no kid in his house was going to be defenseless in a card game. Plus, it gave us something to do when we were stuck together. He used to set me up to fleece his friends."

"Now she fleeces *my* friends," Cade said from his seat by the window. It was hard not to be at least a little intimidated by the sheer size of the sheriff. For the most part, he'd kept his distance, but he'd offered her reassuring smiles until the doctor told them Rick was going to be fine. Katrina, however, wasn't nearly as reticent. She'd hugged Whitney right away, helped her get changed from the bloody nightgown into scrubs one of the nurses had dug up. The gown had gone into an evidence bag, but Whitney still held the small blue memory card. She'd slipped it into her bra before heading back to Rick and Alison. Now it was burning a hole in her palm. It was the last, most important piece of the puzzle.

It was time to be rid of it.

Whitney stood up, quietly crossing to Cade. He took his feet off the chair there, giving her access to the window seat. His brown eyes curious, he stayed silent until she could open her hand and offered him the card. "Please, keep this between us, if you can. It's…" She wasn't sure she could explain. "It's what started this."

And it would end it, too. Finally, it would end.

"I'll let Rick know you have it," she added, because Cade had to know she wasn't asking him to lie. The same way she wouldn't ask Rick to, not even to defend her. This was her secret, her nightmare. She had to be the one to kill it. "All I ask is that you don't make him watch it. He shouldn't have to go through that again."

He looked down at the small card in his very large hand, then back to her. "All right." He studied her, probably taking in the scratches from the bushes and trees. But, no, she realized he was looking deeper than that. "Are you sure you're okay? What happened out there, it's a lot to deal with."

She looked down at her hands. They were knotted together on her lap. "I did what I had to do." What Alison meant her to do, she knew. A final manipulation.

"Just because we have to, doesn't mean it sits right with us."

She met his gaze again, not wanting him to think less of her. There was only kindness in his eyes. He glanced at Rick and she knew he meant more. Like Rick, he knew about choices that weren't choices. And the price they exacted.

"Alison was *my* responsibility. He shouldn't have to carry that weight, too."

"Can *you* carry it?"

She had to. If Rick had been the one to shoot, he would expect her to hate him for it, no matter what she said. It would have been a poison, just like Alison wanted. She wasn't ready to think too much about the broken girl or what she'd had to do, but she did know there was no other choice. Alison would have killed him. There wasn't a single doubt in her mind about that. The same way Alison would have killed Whitney.

"My life wouldn't be worth living without him." It was the only explanation she had to give him. Cade's smile, gentle as it was, transformed his face. Naturally stern and somewhat forbidding, she could understand now why his wife sometimes looked at him and blushed.

"Whit?" Rick's graveled voice had them both jumping to their feet. By the time she got to his side, his eyes were open. Bleary, but open.

"Right here," she said, taking his hand. He blinked at her a few times, then looked over to see his father, Cade, and Katrina surrounding his feet. The latter winked.

"Don't you ever get tired of catching bullets?" Katrina asked sweetly.

"Who the hell let *you* into my room?" A faint smile creased his cheeks.

"Same crazy man who saved your dumb ass." She hooked a thumb at his father.

Richard shrugged, his eyes glistening when Rick turned his way. "She seemed nice enough in the hall." Not a word about how he'd come running, how he'd struggled to treat

Rick until the paramedics had been able to take over. But that was Richard. Just one of the many ways Rick took after him.

"I think he loves me more than you now," Katrina added, her teasing grin covering the worry Whitney had seen on the other woman's face since arriving at the hospital hours ago. She'd been a godsend as far as keeping Richard occupied, especially when Whitney had to give a statement while Rick was being worked on.

"Quit hitting on my father." Rick's hand curled around Whitney's, tight and strong. She released a relieved breath, wanting nothing more than to climb into that bed with him and hold him. He looked over at her, almost as if he couldn't believe she was there.

"How about we give the two of them a little privacy?" Richard suggested with a cough. Cade and Katrina agreed, Katrina squeezing Rick's ankle briefly. Cade offered a nod that Rick smiled tiredly at.

"Dad?" he asked when Richard was almost to the door. His father turned expectantly. "You'll come back soon, right?"

She saw the older man swallow the lump in his throat and nod as well, then he, too, left the room. Once the door was closed, she lowered the rail and climbed up on the bed, nuzzling into his uninjured side. She had to touch him, feel for herself that he was safe. That they both were. His arm came around her just as urgently, so she figured he didn't mind.

"I can't believe you came back for me," he rumbled. It wasn't his pleased rumble, either, despite his lips against her forehead.

"I wasn't leaving you there to die." She wasn't apologizing, either.

But he seemed to want to. "About Alison…"

She shook her head.

"We have to talk about this. I don't want you to—"

"I knew what I was doing," she interrupted. "What she was doing, too. I won't let her twist saving you into something I'd ever regret. Loving you, choosing *you*, is one thing in my life I've done right. You don't get to feel guilty about it."

He studied her face. "You love me."

She thought about making a fuss concerning what he paid attention to, but then she just shook her head. "Yes, you idiot. I love you. So much that I thought I'd die when you… When you…"

He settled a finger over her lips. "Okay."

She peered up at him. "*Okay?*"

"I'm learning to accept." Grudgingly, it seemed.

"Did that concussion scramble your personality, too?"

"Not as much as you'd like." So, not at all, then. He tried again, "I do listen to you. I don't always agree, but I'm listening."

"I know." If he didn't, they wouldn't argue as much. "Just don't expect me to let you sacrifice yourself for me. I need you too much."

"I think I finally understand that."

"Don't forget it." Ever. "Sleep. I'll be here when you wake up."

"There's a lot to talk about still," he reminded tiredly.

"Nothing that can't wait."

He must have decided she was right because they drifted into silence so long she thought he'd dozed off again. "You scared the life out of me," he admitted, startling her. "Don't ever do anything like that again, Whit. Please."

Much as she wished she could make that promise, she knew she wouldn't. Wherever their lives took them, she had every intention of protecting him, the same way she knew he'd protect her. "Yeah, well, you returned the favor, so we're even."

"We are not *remotely* even." It would have sounded like a threat but she knew him too well.

"Fine, I'll let you make it up to me then." For the rest of their very long lives, if she had anything to say about it. And she absolutely planned to.

His laugh, she decided then, had to be the best sound in the whole wide world.

Epilogue

She slept. Peacefully. Her back curved into his chest, their legs tangled comfortably. Rick watched her in silence, the glow from the night-light across the room bathing her bare shoulder.

She'd come a long way since Alison's death, moving into his house by tacit agreement right out of the hospital. She hadn't wanted to be alone and he didn't want her to be, simple as that. It was probably the only simple thing they'd faced.

Back then, the only way she'd been able to sleep had been with every light in the room on, eradicating every shadow. Little by little, she'd been making progress, the therapist she'd found helping her in ways Rick knew he never could. But, he also knew he helped her as well.

He'd gotten in the habit of waking often to make

sure she wasn't suffering another night terror. At the first whimper, he did his best to soothe her, remind her that she was safe and protected. Some nights that worked, others the dreams dug in their teeth and all he could do was hold her in the aftermath. But she wasn't alone and after a while, that seemed to make a difference.

It had been weeks since the last one, but he still woke up to check. To assure himself that she was all right. Every day, she seemed happier and more settled than the last. It wasn't just her smiles, or the shadows fading from her eyes bit by bit. He could see it in his house, which had become more and more of a home since she'd come into it. There was bakeware in his kitchen now, plants and herbs by his windows, and small feminine touches in every room. Even that scent of cinnamon and sweetness he'd always attributed to her. There were pictures now, too. On the walls, on the tables. He'd come home one night to find her and his father pouring over albums and ancient looking shoeboxes full of memories. Next thing he knew, they were everywhere.

She'd even managed to dig out his military memorabilia, turning the spartan den he used for an office into a space marked with his past as well as his present. She'd worried, afraid maybe she'd overstepped but, being Whitney, she did it anyway. He was surprised to realize how much it meant to him, to see all the things he'd put away as if they belonged to someone else. The only thing he hadn't been ready for was the picture she'd found of him and his unit in Afghanistan. They'd been smiling that day, laughing at something Galindo had said about someone's poor, much-maligned mother. All of them looked so young, especially him and Cade.

While he couldn't keep it in the place of honor she'd

created on one of the shelves, he did pull it out of his desk drawer from time to time. It reminded him that not every memory was bad. That the four men deserved to be remembered for the lives they'd lived, not their deaths. A reminder he'd somehow started to accept.

Someday, they'd be up on that shelf. When it was time.

He tugged the blankets up over Whitney's shoulder, pressing a kiss to her neck as he did. It was time for other things now. Time to heal, to move forward with their lives. Not to forget, according to Whitney's therapist who saw them together each week, but maybe…to forgive. He wasn't ready for that step just yet, but he understood why Whitney liked the woman so much. She didn't dress anything up with pithy mumbo-jumbo or answer questions with more questions. She talked to them about reasoning solutions out for themselves. He could work with reason.

Unfortunately, reason wasn't what was chanting in the back of his mind right then. What he wanted had pretty much nothing to do with reason and everything to do with him being an impatient jackass. Considering Whitney had waited literally decades for him to wake up and see how much she meant to him, now that he did know, all he wanted to do was make sure everyone else did too. To know she belonged to him and he, finally, belonged to her.

If anything, the want had become a need.

The week before, both he and Cade had taken a rare night off together, Whitney inviting him and Katrina—and of course, Richard—because she claimed she was itching to make a big family dinner. He thought maybe she was just itching to spend some time with Katrina and maybe even to get her hands on the other woman's expanding belly.

Katrina's pregnancy had surprised everyone—possibly the woman, herself, most—but Whitney never passed up a chance to coax the baby to kick her hand.

He'd been sitting on the couch, listening to Katrina and his father talking, when Cade walked behind his wife's chair, his hand absently landing on her shoulder. Katrina had been laughing, both hands on her stomach, but she looked up at Cade and the brief, intimate smile they shared was a testament to the strength of their bond. He'd looked at Whitney, but she was watching them, too. Not with jealousy, but he could see the longing in her eyes.

Whitney stirred, her lashes lifting as if they were almost too heavy to keep open. It took her a few seconds to realize he was awake, but when she did, she turned her body to face him. Sleep deepened her voice as she resettled, nuzzling into his chest. "Something wrong?"

Yes. She wasn't telling him something, something important. "I'm not sure. What do you think?"

She peered up at him, one eye scrunching shut. "I'm not the one laying awake in the dark. Or, at least, I *wasn't*."

He smiled, sinking his hand in her hair, just to feel the curls wrap around it. His Whitney, never too sleepy for sass. Probably not for honesty, either. "I want to ask you something, but I'm worried it's too soon."

"Hmmm. Well, since icebergs are speedsters compared to you, there's a chance you might be wrong." She shifted, definitely awake now, so she could take what seemed to be her favorite position of halfway laying across his chest. Just like always, her hand found a place over his heartbeat, her chin right above. "Must be bad to have you worrying."

Was it? "The other night, I saw you looking at Cade and

Katrina."

Her eyes gave away that she knew what he was talking about.

"You're missing something, aren't you?"

She shrugged. "Yes and no. They seem…so happy together. And they have so much to be excited about. But she's worried what kind of mother she'll be."

Well, that wasn't what he expected. "She'll be the most protective mother on the planet."

"It made me think of my mother, how much she missed out on." That was the wistfulness.

"How much *you've* missed out on?" Most people their age had married a while ago, some of them with children in grade school, even.

"How much I have to look forward to," she corrected with a teasing grin, her fingers pinching his chest. "One hopes, anyway."

Yes, one did. But like all the hopes she'd taught him to believe in again, this one depended on her. "Are you happy here with me?"

Even in the half dark, he saw her eyes widen. "You can't tell?"

She seemed like it, she truly did. But now he'd find out for sure. He tucked an errant curl behind her ear, smoothing his thumb over her cheek. "Happy enough to stay?"

Her body seemed to melt against him, her smile softening on her lips as she relaxed. "I suppose I could… How long are we talking?"

He didn't hesitate. "Forever."

She closed her eyes, breathing in slowly, looking almost as if she were…savoring something.

"Whit?"

"Shhh." She tapped his chest with a reprimanding finger. "Just let me…"

He waited, but she stayed silent, unmoving. Long enough to make him scowl. "Let you what?"

One of her eyes opened. Irritably, he rather thought. "I've been waiting thirty years for this moment, Trelane. You do not get to rush through it."

"According to you, I don't know how to rush." And sometimes, panting and shaking with erotic satisfaction, she seemed pretty ecstatic about that quality.

"You have your moments," she replied, lips twitching.

He sighed. She couldn't even let him do *this* without yanking his chain. And God, he hoped that never stopped. Cupping her face, he leaned forward and stole a kiss. A full on, need-you-now, don't-ever-go kind of kiss that ended with her rolled beneath him. Giggling. "Woman, I'm trying to be serious here."

That made her laugh harder. And damn it, he was laughing now, too.

That's how he knew this was the right time. Looking down at her, the joy on her face lighting his entire world, it was finally time. "Marry me, Whitney."

She made a sound he'd remember for the rest of his life. Hopefully into eternity. A whisper of a sigh, pure and feminine, a balm and a blessing all at once. "Yes."

Whitney pulled him down for a kiss, gentle and sweet. It started that way, anyway, just like everything about their lives together had. Then it bloomed into something that filled him, heart and soul. He didn't have the words to define it, still wasn't completely sure he deserved it, but he knew he couldn't live another day without it.

Five years it had taken him, since the day he'd dragged Cade to the side of that fiery road and returned for the dead. Five long, painful years, feeling he was still there with them. To his amazement, to his eternal gratefulness, he'd finally made it back, led there by the same hand that held him so steady now, that loved him. That would always hold his heart.

He was home.

About the Author

Dee Tenorio has a few reality issues. After much therapy for the problem--if one can call being awakened in the night by visions of hot able-bodied men a problem--she has proved incurable. It turns out she enjoys tormenting herself by writing sizzling, steamy romances of various genres spanning paranormal mystery dramas, contemporaries and romantic comedies. Preferably starring the sexy, somewhat grumpy heroes described above and smart-mouthed heroines who have much better hair than she does. The best part is, no more therapy bills! Well, not for Dee, anyway. Her husband and kids, on the other hand…

Also by Dee Tenorio…

CONVICTED